A LOVELY
TOMORROW

A LOVELY TOMORROW

Mabel Esther Allan

DODD, MEAD & COMPANY

New York

EC. Read march 1995
a good story.

1   2   3   4   5   6   7   8   9   10

Library of Congress Cataloging in Publication Data

Allan, Mabel Esther.
A lovely tomorrow.

SUMMARY: After her parents are killed by a rocket on New
Year's Eve in London, 15-year-old Frue rebuilds her life in the
wartime English countryside.
[1. Orphans—Fiction. 2. England—Fiction. 3. World War,
1939-1945—Great Britain—Fiction]
I. Title.
PZ7.A4Lo   1980   [Fic]   79-6642
ISBN 0-396-07813-3

This book is dedicated to all those people, both adults and girls, who were there in the Chiltern Hills in 1945. They would not, maybe, recognize themselves, but they helped suggest this story. And the great house is really there, but with another name.

Contents

1

Prelude

When war was coming we went to Cornwall. It was late August, 1939, and I was nine, going on ten. Father said we might as well keep to our plans; it would be the last holiday we would have in a long time, maybe ever.

We chose Cornwall because we had some neighbors in Chelsea, the Tremartins, who had originally come from there and they often talked about it. Father thought that, if the world didn't end soon, he might make a film about Cornwall, and it would be good to spy out the land. In those days he was an up-and-coming film director, mainly of documentaries, though he had recently made his name in Britain with a strange little film shot in the Chiltern Hills northwest of London. *Traveler's Joy* was a story, a kind of ghost story, and I had a part in it. Quite a big part, as the little ghost child, Joy. My name was there in the cast line, Fruella Allendale.

For our Cornish holiday we had rented a cottage at Kennack Sands on the Lizard peninsula in the south-west. I had started to keep a diary by then, so I have something to help me, but I remember it all vividly. I remember the summer air . . . running on the sand at sunset, with a full moon rising . . . walking high on the earthen banks that take the place of hedges on the Lizard.

I remember Mother saying, "John, if war does come, how do you think it will affect us?"

"War will come, Kate," Father answered. We had been in Cornwall for a week and the news was worse each day. "And, when it does, nothing will ever be the same again. I suppose I will be called up. With luck I may be able to do the same job in the Army. They'll need film makers. That's what I hope, anyway."

"And us?" Mother asked. She was twenty-nine then. They had married when she was just eighteen. She was very pretty, with red hair and a clear, pale skin. She was sitting on a bank among the blowing grasses. The wind was hot and sweet.

I remember that I didn't believe any of it. War. . . . What was war to us? Russia and Germany seemed so far away. The only reality then was summer, and Cornish coves and the strange inland country that had such a haunting quality. The ancient standing stones, with their secret power, scared me.

Reality in London was our house in a Chelsea mews, and the Lennox Stage School that I had been attending for nearly a year.

"You and Frue couldn't stay in London, Kate. It will be a target for the enemy."

"I shall stay in London," said my mother. She had been born not quite within the sound of Bow bells, but in Hammersmith.

The next day we went to St. Mawes, and then, by small boat, to St. Anthony-in-Roseland. There was an old stone manor house dreaming among late roses, and a bare headland with a lighthouse. We were very cheerful; I was wildly happy. It was all so glorious. I think I gave some of my heart to Cornwall then, though the country, to me, was just somewhere to visit. Never, oh, never, to live in.

But by evening the news on the radio was worse. We sat in the garden of the cottage, while the full moon bathed the whole scene in silver light. Close by was a farmyard, and I climbed the bank and sat at the foot of a haystack with kittens all around me. They were mostly gray kittens, ghostly in the moonlight. It was hot and still, and I could hear the wash of the tide on the beach. When I went back Father was saying, "We had better go home tomorrow. We can't avoid the issue any longer."

So we drove home. In Plymouth the barrage balloons were floating over the town, like great fat whales, faintly shining. The first sign of preparation for what was to come. It was Friday, September 1. The news stands were displaying such slogans as: "Evacuation. Children leave major cities."

I felt scared and vaguely excited. I said, "I won't be evacuated. I'm not going. You won't make me?"

Mother was silent. Father said, "It's hard to know what's right. You're too young to choose."

"No," I said. "In November I'll be ten. I can choose. You always said I am a person in my own right. So I won't go. Not like those kids in the newspaper pictures, with labels around their necks. I'd sooner die with you than live in the country."

"It wouldn't be labels, Frue," Father answered. "If you were sent away I suppose it would be to your Aunt Mildred in the Chilterns. She's the obvious person. That remote village, Little Hartsthorn. You'd be perfectly safe there. But not too far from London. Only about thirty miles."

That settled it. Aunt Mildred was Mother's aunt, so really my great-aunt. I had seen something of her while we were filming near by, and she had disapproved of the whole project strongly. Father had made a great joke of her. Pillar of the Women's Institute and the local church; conventional to the core. No doubt an admirable woman by some standards, he had said, but not our kind. I knew she wasn't. The very thought of living at Dogwood House was just awful. A widow for many years, Aunt Mildred had clearly bullied her elder, unmarried daughter, Muriel. The younger daughter had run away.

"Anyway, who's going to die?" said Mother, taking up my last remark. Mother always took life lightly until there was real cause for alarm. "We'll probably win the war in three months."

Death meant nothing to me then. Sitting in the front seat beside Father, Mother looked completely alive, her hair blowing brightly in the hot wind that came through the open windows.

Maybe it was already written that she was to die. Or was it chance . . . sheer chance?

"People do, in war," Father said. "There'll be air raids, perhaps at once. But we brought Frue up to be independent. If the Lennox School is evacuated she had better go with them. On second thought, that would be better than Aunt Mildred. Otherwise she'll stay in London."

I stayed in London, though the war was not over in three months. Half the Lennox School was evacuated to Wiltshire, but the other half remained. At first in its usual home north of Regent's Park; then later, when the building was bombed, it moved to South Kensington.

Father was called up, and he did make documentaries for the Army. Mother was an air raid warden, and was often out patroling the Chelsea streets at night. Throughout all the bombing our little house was quite untouched, apart from broken windows. I was often scared, but I never wished to go away. Aunt Mildred occasionally descended on us, bearing wonderful things from the country—a chicken, apples, raspberries—and said it was wicked to keep a child in the city.

The child, me, flourished and grew in that strange world of danger and privation. I did well at the Lennox School and had a small part in a London play when I was fourteen. The play didn't run for long, but I received good notices.

D Day came, in early June, 1944, and our troops landed in Normandy. Some day the war might be over, but I couldn't imagine a world where there was no danger. The Germans sent over the V1s, which were nastier than ordinary bombs, in a way. They were unmanned aircraft, and when they cut out directly above you, you knew you were for it. After these came the rockets, the V2s; worse still, because they arrived without warning. But still life went on. I went to school every day, regardless of what had happened during the night. Then I began to attend rehearsals again, for I had a very small part in another West End play that was to open soon after the New Year.

"Your father will be home for Christmas," Mother told me, after reading his latest letter, heavily censored. He was somewhere in Northern France. "Christmas

Eve, he hopes." Her eyes shone and she went upstairs to cut out a new dress from a green curtain she had bought at a rummage sale after a free fight. We were both dreadfully short of clothes by then. Clothing coupons didn't go far, and any kind of material was like gold.

"We'll have a little party on New Year's Eve, Frue," she said, when I looked around the door to find her crawling about the floor, her hair untidy. "My birthday, and your father home. . . ." I knew she was still in love with my father. It seemed strange, when they were both in their thirties. That seemed pretty old to me, in a way, though she looked about twenty down on the floor, smiling up at me.

"What's it like to love someone?" I asked. I turned away to stare in the mirror in her dressing table. I wished I were as good looking as she was. I was too thin, and my face looked pale and bony. But my nose and mouth were all right, and I had reddish tints in my hair.

I was fifteen and I really had no experience of love. I knew plenty of boys at school, and one or two had made passes at me. The only boy I had ever felt a little attracted to was Paul Tremartin. The Tremartins lived down the mews, and they were the Cornish family I mentioned in the beginning. Paul was nearly three years older than I was, and once he used to tease me, but now he didn't take much notice of me. Too old and grand. He was a senior at a famous London day school, and would soon be leaving.

"Hell and heaven," said my mother, snipping at the old curtain. "I'm afraid only clichés describe it. You'll find out."

Aunt Mildred turned up two days before Christmas,

14

with a rabbit and a chicken, fresh from the country. And a basket of apples that had been stored in her loft. She actually had an orchard of her own. There was also a small cheese, illicitly made on a farm. They were supposed to send all their milk away.

"So we won't starve," Mother said. There was almost nothing in the shops, and our only bonus at Christmas was half a pound of sugar and half a pound of margarine.

"Frue looks as if she is," Aunt Mildred said tartly. "You should have sent that child to me years ago. I would have given her a better life than she's had in London. She could have helped Muriel in the house and done some gardening. But you and John always were obstinate. Marrying a man who makes films, and letting Frue have ridiculous ideas about acting."

Mother didn't answer. I said, "I *am* an actress, and someday I'll be good. I have a part in another play. Just a little part. It opens on January 7." I was scared of Aunt Mildred because she always seemed formidable in her old clothes and country shoes. She had a way of looking at me that made me feel about eight. But I tried to stand up to her.

We were both glad when she left. She was kind after her fashion, and the food was real treasure. She had had a horrible bus and train journey in bad weather to bring it, but her presence cast a blight in our very different world.

Father came home and we had a wonderful Christmas, even though the weather was pretty awful and a rocket fell two streets away, near the King's Road. He had brought two bottles of wine and said we must keep them for the New Year's Eve party. There was hardly anything to drink in London. The pubs had to close on Christmas Day.

"I shall have to get drunk with joy, that's all," Father said. Actually he hardly ever drank at all. He was already making plans for when the war was over, though getting started again in films wasn't going to be easy. He had almost no money saved. They always talked in front of me and treated me as if I were a really sensible human being. They did even when I was little.

Mother had finished the green dress and it looked splendid. When the war began she could hardly sew on a button. My buttons were always falling off again after her attempts. Now she was clever. She had also made me a velvet skirt, out of the good bits of an old evening dress of hers, and given up precious coupons to buy me a blouse. It was royal blue, with long sleeves; very grown up.

Five people came to our New Year's Eve party; the three Tremartins and two other neighbors. They were all "our kind of people." Mr. Tremartin was an artist before the war, and he was just establishing a reputation when the war began. Once they lived at St. Ives in Cornwall, then moved to London. He was a little lame, but had to take a wartime job, though he kept on painting in his spare time. I was vaguely scared of his pictures. The wartime ones were all of broken buildings, or fires caused by the bombing. I had seen plenty of scenes like that in reality but, strangely, his paintings seemed more frightening.

I had thought maybe Paul wouldn't come, though he was asked. Someone so grown up and sophisticated would probably have other parties to go to on New

16

Year's Eve. But the party he was going to was put off because of rocket damage, and he came to us. He was very tall, with a pale, clever face, and he wore the most dreadful old trousers and sweater. His school clothes were kept strictly for school.

He came into the kitchen with me while I was assembling the food we had managed to raise for the guests. Not much, but they were used to that, and Mr. Tremartin had had two glasses of wine and was too cheerful even to notice what he ate. Like my father, he cared more about good talk than his stomach. It wasn't really the wine made him cheerful . . . I knew that.

I was excited. I had been listening to the conversation, which I always loved. Talk about films, and art, and the theatre. For they hadn't left me out. They had never really forgotten I was there. The one who was almost entirely silent was Paul. He always was a quiet boy, kind of remote. He was not artistic; books were the light of his life. Books and the knowledge they held. Paul was going to be clever in a different way from his father, and never famous, maybe. When the war was over he would be going to Oxford. Imprisoned we had been on our island, Britain, but, when we were free to travel, perhaps Paul could go and see some of those far distant sites he read about, for his passion was ancient civilizations. I knew most of this secondhand.

Paul had been quiet, but he had looked at me. He had been looking at me all evening. That was exciting in itself, and I didn't quite understand it. He had taken so little notice of me for the last two years. Though he had seen the play I was in a few months before. Incredibly, he had come to me as I walked down the mews, over the shiny old cobblestones, and held out his program. "Sign it, please, Frue," he had said. Until then I had not even known he had seen the play, and my part had been so small. Paul's approach had been a brief miracle that I had soon forgotten in the events of each crowded day.

Now, as I assembled plates, coffee cups, and napkins, he suddenly came around the table.

"Frue . . ."

"Yes?"

"Nothing. You look different tonight. Older. It's strange, isn't it? New Year's Eve. In an hour it will be 1945. The year of hope."

"Clichés cover everything," I said, then could have bitten out my tongue. Me being clever; me being awkward. I did not quite know where I stood with that tall person looming over me.

"So they do," he answered, and laughed. And I laughed, and he bent down and kissed me. Only on the cheek, but I began to know then something of love. Or attraction . . . or sex. Sex was a word I hardly ever allowed myself to use, though my parents used it in my hearing. They were "advanced," at least by Aunt Mildred's standards. Maybe by any standards. In spite of the war I had lived a curiously sheltered life. Yes, in a stage school, in London, with plenty of boys. Things "went on," but I was young looking for my age, and thin and rather plain. And I was fastidious, physically.

Only I liked that kiss, and instinct made me raise my mouth toward his. Mother called, "Come on, Frue! We're waiting!"

So we ate and drank coffee, and midnight was almost upon us. We were not the kind to grow sentimental, but

18

as the midnight hour struck from the old grandfather clock, and out in the mews someone shouted, "Happy New Year! All the best for 1945!" Father poured the last of the wine into all our glasses and we raised them, smiling at each other.

Nineteen forty-five. Everyone said that the war would be over in a few months. Mr. Tremartin would paint pictures that were different from those flaring, tragic ones. . . . Father would make wonderful films. . . . I would go on learning to be an actress. Money would come from somewhere to make it all possible. And Paul was living near, and one day I would be older.

"Happy New Year!"

Within an hour that part of my life was over, and I thought I would never be happy again.

2

When the Dust Cleared

The guests went home a few minutes before one o'clock. We stood on the doorstep, hearing their retreating footsteps ringing on the cobblestones. It was very cold and dark, but there was singing far away, and laughter. In that winter blackout, people were celebrating still.

"Well, at least there were no rockets," Father said. He sat down in his favorite chair in the front room and poured the last drops of wine into Mother's glass.

"We have charmed lives, I think," said Mother dreamily.

"Touch wood! Oh, touch wood!" I cried, and Mother laughed. But she reached out to touch the old oak table.

Mother sat down opposite Father and drank the wine. Her eyes were very bright. I caught the glance they exchanged and my heart gave a strange little lurch. I knew that, when they went to bed, they would make love. I didn't really understand, but I didn't mind. I knew love when I saw it, and lived with it. I knew how desperately they missed each other when apart.

"I'll clear away a bit," I said. "You just sit for a minute."

"Bed for you, Frue," Father suggested.

"Soon. I don't have to get up early." I carried the cups

and saucers, plates and glasses into the kitchen and piled them up neatly to wait until morning. I had closed the door between us, but I could hear the murmur of their voices. I was happy, humming to myself.

There were a lot of crumbs. I went quickly out into the tiny back garden, shutting the outer door behind me so as not to show any light. That was habit. It didn't matter so much showing a light now that the Germans sent different weapons. Scattering the crumbs in the darkness for the sparrows in the morning, I drew a deep breath of the cold air.

I was filled with a kind of wild elation, an extra feeling of being alive. I remembered Paul's kiss and the way I had turned up my mouth, and the future seemed to hold all kinds of promises. We, a happy family, with my father home again, and . . .

Like an axe falling . . . like the end of the world. All at once unbearable noise and crashing sounds, and my eardrums bursting. And there I was against the far brick wall, winded, gasping, lying on the winter earth where nothing much grew even in summer.

Sometimes you could hear the whine of the rockets *after* they fell. Some curious fact of the speed of sound. But I didn't hear anything after that first burst of terrible noise. I was deaf and shaken and gasping for life after the blast. But I certainly wasn't dead.

I got to my feet somehow, and my breath came back enough for me to grope my way blindly toward the back door of the house. The air was filled with dust and smoke and I fell over the door before I had gone far.

Maybe I was screaming. I could only think of my father and mother. Getting to them . . . finding them safe.

22

The kitchen seemed still there; at least the way was fairly clear. The light switch didn't work, but I was led by a red glare through the space where the inner door had been. Then I was in the living room, where the dust was clearing. Perhaps I had been longer than a minute or so recovering from the blast.

The whole front of our little house had gone, and across the mews, where there had been a large house behind a high wall, a fire was burning strongly. The red light showed me the remains of our living room, and, by some strange quirk of blast, my parents still sitting in their chairs opposite each other. The wine glasses had been flung across the room and one was rolling near my feet, unbroken.

My father and mother were dead, quite dead, still sitting there. My mother wearing the green dress she had made for Father's homecoming and her birthday; her hair brighter than ever in the light of the fire.

The ceiling was sagging over them, and over me. I stood there, feeling as if it were I who was dead. A ghost, who couldn't hear. But hearing began to come back, and I heard the crackle of the fire and shouts outside in the mews. Then Mr. Tremartin and Paul appeared in the red glare and saw me and those two sitting in their chairs under the ceiling that was going to fall any minute, burying us all.

"Get them out!" I screamed. Yes, I could scream, quite logically, too.

Mr. Tremartin came in and said, "They're dead, Frue. Come out quickly, dear. Take her, Paul."

Paul tried to drag me, not very gently. I resisted and my foot came up against something. I looked down and it was my diary; the big, thick diary, really a gilt-edged notebook, that had been given to me when I was nine years old. Each year since was in that book; sometimes only tiny entries, with large spaces between.

I bit Paul's hand so that he would release me and bent and grabbed my book. I felt almost nothing then, but later I thought I was rescuing what was left of my life. I had been writing in the book before the party.

Paul again tried to drag me, but again I resisted. I wanted to stay with my parents; then, when the ceiling fell, I would be dead, too.

But they got me out, and there were ambulances and wardens and police. The house that had actually been hit was an inferno by then. Dimly I heard voices saying that everyone must be dead; the firemen could do nothing. There had been several flats in the house. "Must have had oil heaters for it to go up like that," said a young policeman.

I remember standing there in the mews. In the glare I could see that the Tremartins' house, at the end, was not very much damaged, though there was a hole in the roof of the studio and the glass had gone from every window. Mrs. Tremartin was there, crying. She was still wearing the dress she had worn for our party.

"What ought we to do with the girl?" one of the policemen asked, and, at that moment, more of our little house collapsed behind me. Burying my father and mother, but they would get them out later. Coughing in the dust and smoke, wishing to be dead, too, I could say nothing. But I heard Mr. Tremartin answer, "There's a great crack in the side of our house. Can you find us a taxi? We'll go to a hotel for the rest of the night. I'll take Frue Allendale."

"The hotels are pretty full," the policeman said doubtfully. "People came for New Year's, in spite of the rockets. No accounting for tastes," he added. He looked as if he were going to be sick. I would know him if I met him today. I shall never forget his face, seen in those moments of horror.

A taxi was found for us and we drove through London to Piccadilly Circus. Most of the New Year crowds had gone by then, though a few drunks lay around the boarded-up statue of Eros. We went to the Regent Palace Hotel, just off the Circus. A night porter standing at the main door hesitated when he saw us. We must have looked drunk or something. Dusty, strange and unsuitable.

"We've had a rocket in Chelsea," Mr. Tremartin explained. "I know the manager. He's a friend of mine. We want three rooms for the rest of the night."

"I don't think there are any," said the porter, but he let us in. The hotel was as bright as midday, with people still milling around the entrance hall and sitting in the great lounge. Though it was by then nearly two in the morning, the manager was still up and available. Mr. Tremartin really did know him, and, by some miracle, rooms were found for us. Mine was very small and looked out on the shaft, or deep well, in the center of the great hotel. I stood by the window thinking maybe I *was* dead. Mr. Tremartin came in with something in a small glass.

"Brandy, Frue," he said. "Drink it, love. Then get into bed."

"I have no pajamas . . . nothing," I said, backing away from the glass.

"Never mind that. Drink this."

"I shall be sick." My teeth were chattering.

"Then be sick, dear girl. But you must have something."

I drank the brandy. There was only a very little, but it burned my throat, already sore from the dust and smoke. I coughed until my eyes watered, but there was warmth in my cold and awful stomach.

"Would you like Lulwyn to come and stay with you?"

Lulwyn was Mrs. Tremartin. Very nice, with a Cornish voice; born in Penzance of a fishing family. But I didn't want anyone.

"No, thank you."

"I'm going to telephone your aunt, Frue," he said. "Mrs. Butler—Mildred Butler, isn't she? Lives somewhere in the Chiltern Hills?"

"Dogwood House, Little Hartsthorn," I heard myself saying. Then I realized what he meant. "I don't *want* Aunt Mildred! Please don't telephone her in the middle of the night. I can't *bear* Aunt Mildred, and she'll be asleep . . ."

"Look," he said, and put his hands on my shoulders, "have you any other relations?"

I shook my head. I had none. My parents had both been only children, and *their* parents were dead.

"Then it has to be your Aunt Mildred. I'll just tell her what has happened. No one has petrol. She can't drive here. But in the morning she can come by train."

The whole nightmare thing rose up and hit me anew.

"Who will get my father and mother out? What will they do with them? Oh, I *am* dreaming!" I clutched Mr. Tremartin. "I *will* wake up, won't I?"

Mr. Tremartin was pretty tall. He looked down at me with great compassion in his face. "You are awake, Frue. It did happen. You have to face it. It has happened to other people all through the war."

But we had charmed lives; my mother had said so. She had even touched wood, an absurd superstition that clearly didn't work. Of course I knew of plenty of stories. There was a girl at school who had survived when three brothers had died with her parents. There was a boy who had lost everyone but a baby sister, who had been dug out of the rubble alive after three days. But I had never for one moment thought it could happen to me.

"If I hadn't gone out at the back to scatter crumbs I'd be dead, too," I said.

"Be thankful you went," he said.

"How can I be? I don't want to be alive all alone. They were going to bed together. They were in love." I gasped and nearly choked. "We had all kinds of plans for when the war is over. You know; you were there. I *hate* 1945!"

He kissed me on the cheek and left me. I suddenly saw myself in the mirror and hardly knew that strange, white-faced apparition. My hair and my beautiful royal blue blouse were dusty, and my skirt had a big tear in it. My hands were bleeding a little, and I suddenly realized that they hurt.

I took off all my clothes, washed my face and hands and fell into bed. The sheets were very crisp, as if they were new. Not like our old, torn linen ones from prewar.

An hour later a rocket landed not far away. I heard the whine of its coming echoing strangely in the well of the hotel *after* it had arrived. Yet people were still awake and laughing. I heard some merrymakers coming along the corridor a few minutes later. Death was hovering; far away Germans were manning those rocket ranges in a last desperate effort to win the war. But people in London could laugh. *We* had been laughing only a few hours ago.

3

I Go to Little Hartsthorn

Aunt Mildred arrived at nine o'clock. I went down to the hotel lounge to meet her. Mrs. Tremartin had lent me a comb, and a chambermaid produced a clothes brush. The only possession I had was my diary, which I held tightly under my arm. Its hard edges pressed into me and were a curious kind of comfort.

The lounge was deserted at that hour, dimly lit and with faint, cold daylight coming through the stained-glass windows. No one had cleaned it, and ashtrays were overflowing. Tattered paper hats lay on the floor, sad remains of New Year merrymaking.

The Tremartins accompanied me. Paul, still wearing the dreadful sweater, whispered to me, "Bear up, Frue! She'll take you away, but I won't forget you. I'll see you again . . . I promise. I'll think of something, or Dad will."

Aunt Mildred looked awful. She had crammed on her old, heavy clothes just anyhow, and she looked much older than usual. Maybe I did, too. I felt a hundred and one. She and Mr. and Mrs. Tremartin talked; I sat in a deep chair and wished I had not eaten a piece of toast and drunk a cup of tea. Any minute I would have to run away and be sick. Through my physical discomfort I heard Aunt Mildred say, "I'd better take the girl straight back

29

with me. She's in a state of shock, anyone can see. I would be very grateful if you could find out . . . make arrangements. I'll come back tomorrow. Where can I reach you? Maybe your telephone isn't working. Well, perhaps you'd telephone me later, when you know more. This is a terrible business, but at least Frue is alive."

No, I thought, I am not alive, Aunt Mildred. And I know you resent and do not understand artists. You are not "our kind," Aunt Mildred. You came, you are doing your duty; I ought to be grateful, but I hate you.

I hadn't even a coat, but she had brought one. Mr. Tremartin must have explained. The coat belonged to Muriel and was so large it swamped me, but I was glad of its warm folds as I stood out on the pavement in the icy air, while the doorman tried to get us a taxi.

January, 1945 . . . the year of hope. And my life had ended; the one I knew. On the corner up near Piccadilly Circus a street musician was playing "It's a Lovely Day Tomorrow." The evocative tune was unbearable.

At the last moment it was Mrs. Tremartin to whom I clung. She was warm and kind and a lot cleverer than you might expect someone from a simple fishing family to be, and she had been dealing with her husband and Paul for all those years.

"I do wish I were dead, too," I whispered.

"You won't wish it in time, Frue," she said. "You'll find a new life. You were made for living. I've always thought you have enormous potential, and your father and mother were proud of you."

"I won't find a new life with Aunt Mildred," I murmured shakily.

"You might learn something different. She means well. Be kind to her."

Be kind to *her*. I wanted to scratch Aunt Mildred's eyes out, and the eyes of the whole world. Underneath Muriel's dreadful coat was my velvet skirt and the royal-blue blouse given to me with such love and joy. Less than twelve hours ago my father and mother were alive, and laughing, and loving each other and me.

But I could still think of the Tremartins and their own troubles. They had been so kind to me, and I had always liked them next best to my parents.

"I hope your house isn't too badly damaged, and the studio."

"We'll get it fixed. You'll see it again one day, Frue."

Then Aunt Mildred and I were in a taxi and speeding through London to Baker Street Station. I sat huddled in a corner, dull, sick, and resentful. A hammer was beating in my head, and I was shivering violently. I realized I didn't know where they had taken my father and mother. That was what Aunt Mildred had meant . . . Mr. Tremartin would find out and let her know. There would be a funeral, and I would have to go. I *meant* to go.

I wanted to shout that I wouldn't go with Aunt Mildred into that country world away from the war, where there were still chickens and rabbits and apples stored away in lofts. But I couldn't even speak one word, and she bustled me somehow into the complications of the station, where there were so many levels, and bought me a ticket and pushed me into the Great Missencombe train.

And suddenly, strangely, my eyes began to work over-time. My eyes were never the same again. After that I always saw so much more than I did before. Part of me had died and another part come alive.

I saw every detail of Aunt Mildred as she sat on the other side of the dusty compartment. Her face was deeply lined, but it had a hard, craggy life. She had a big nose and hazel eyes and untidy gray hair. I had seen her many times but never so clearly. She was a human being, and I had never thought of her as real before, just a joke. I was safe from her while Father could laugh at her as the President of the Women's Institute, and as the domi-nator of the village and of her daughter Muriel. Now I was in her power.

Muriel . . . her shabby old coat scratched my neck. Nearly forty and under her mother's thumb. She had not even been allowed to join one of the Women's Services and see life in wartime. Aunt Mildred had got her off, for, at one point of the war, she had had ten evacuees in her house. She had needed Muriel, poor Muriel, and the most her daughter had been able to do outside her home was to join the local Red Cross.

Aunt Mildred imprisoned people. Be kind to her . . . that was a laugh. One might as well try to be kind to a rock on a mountain. I saw her face engraved in stone, part of a great crag, with a blue sky behind it. Perhaps I was delirious.

My newly seeing eyes ranged over the other people in the compartment. There was a young soldier, wearing a shabby greatcoat . . . a young mother with a baby . . . an old man with a rank pipe. They were talking about the rockets that fell on London last night, but they had not been near one. They had not seen the dust and smoke and two people sitting dead. My mother with red hair, in a green dress.

The others had all gone before we reached Great Missencombe. For the last twenty minutes or so we had the compartment to ourselves and sat in silence. Now we were in Buckinghamshire, close to the lovely Chiltern Hills where the film had been made. They were not very beautiful on that cold New Year's Day, or so I thought at first. But something about the curves of the hills and the great black beechwoods comforted me a little. The fields rose up in folds toward the trees, the bare earth plowed into furrows that looked like pale corduroy velvet, almost white. Chalk . . . it was chalk country. Whiter than the chalky fields were the patches of snow lying in hollows. Once, in springtime, I had walked in beechwoods, and acted in them, a child of nine.

Near the train the hedgerows were festooned with a strange, grayish growth, and I suddenly knew what it was. Traveler's-joy, old-man's beard, trailing everywhere. I had only seen it with its flowering little green stars. It had patterned the title shots of Father's film.

I, Joy the ghost child, was traveling with no joy now. I shivered worse than ever, and said across to Aunt Mildred, "I can't stay with you. I go to school in London, you know. And of course I have to go to my parents' funeral." My voice didn't sound like my own.

Aunt Mildred made a strange sound, half a sob and half a snort. But we had reached Great Missencombe. A taxi was waiting outside the station and she pushed me into it. "Little Hartsthorn," she said to the man.

We drove up a long road into the lonely hills. When

33

we came to Hartsthorn Bottom (a row of cottages and a blacksmith's forge) the taxi turned right, up a narrow, winding lane. Little Hartsthorn was at the end of the world. The road didn't go beyond it. Just a path through Hartsthornleaf Wood.

Dogwood House was near the "village." In Buckinghamshire they call it a hamlet. I remembered the house quite well. It was built of brick and flint, with a roof of russet tiles. It was set quite far back from the lane under a curve of the encroaching woods. Now that the woods were closer I could see that they were not black, but held tinges of russet and purple. But the sky was heavy and dark, and snow lay in small gleaming patches in the winter garden.

My eyes saw it all, every detail, while my body shook and my teeth chattered so much that I bit my lip. The pain was startlingly real.

Muriel came around the side of the house. She wore an even older coat than the one covering me, and there was a tattered scarf tied over her head. She wore gum boots caked with mud, and was swinging an empty bucket. With her came three dogs; two setters and a yapping terrier. Father hated dogs and I had caught the feeling from him. We were all "cat" people. We always had cats until halfway through the war.

Muriel put down the bucket, shooed away the dogs, and came forward to me as the taxi drove away. She said, "Frue, dear!" and put her arms briefly around me. She smelled of cold air, wartime soap, and hen food, but she had a nice, warm voice and she was really quite pretty, in spite of being nearly forty.

She started to lead me into the house, but Aunt Mildred said sharply, "Not the front way, Muriel, in those boots!"

"I'll kick them off," Muriel answered, and did so just within the door. The large hall was very cold. No one could heat big places properly. I stood still, with my hands thrust deep into the pockets of Muriel's coat. There were two pennies in one, and a ball of twine in the other.

"We must get her to bed at once," Aunt Mildred said. "Did you warm the bed in the gable room?"

"Oh, yes. There's a hot bottle in it, and I lit a little wood fire. There's some soup . . . won't take a minute. Poor child, she looks very feverish."

"Suffering from shock," Aunt Mildred stated.

"Don't talk about me as if I'm deaf," I said, but my voice came out in a croak. The hammering in my head grew louder, and then the beautifully polished block floor seemed to be coming up to hit me.

The next thing I knew I was in bed, and the room was shadowy, as if it were late afternoon. There was a rosy glow in the firegrate and the faint, sweet smell of wood smoke. There were still hammers in my head and I felt burning hot, so it was strange that I was still shivering.

Suddenly Muriel was bending over me. I was glad it was Muriel and not Aunt Mildred.

"What time is it? Am I ill?" I whispered.

"Four o'clock. Yes, you are a bit ill. The doctor came. He left something for you to take. But first I'll get you some hot milk."

"I can't stay here. I must be in London!"

"You can't be in London yet, Frue, dear. You must rest and sleep."

"My father and mother are dead. Did you know that?"

"Yes," she answered. "I know. Get well, Frue; then we'll talk about it, if you want to."

She gave me some hot milk, then some pills, and I sank again into drowsiness as that New Year's Day died over the Chiltern Hills.

I remember very little of the next few days, but one morning I awoke feeling much better. I had stopped shivering, and my head wasn't hammering, so I sat up, then climbed out of bed and went to the window. My room was at the back of the house and the hills and woods were close. Everywhere was utterly silent in the gray light.

Aunt Mildred came in and caught me standing there with bare feet. She said, "Well, you're better. Put on your dressing gown and slippers, and I'll take you to the bathroom to wash your face. But you mustn't do too much. Stay in bed until the doctor comes."

But memories came rushing back. "What *day* is it?"

"Day? January 6. Now be a good girl and . . ."

January 6. I had lost all those days. I sat down on the bed and stared at Aunt Mildred. She stared back at me and the early light wasn't kind to her face. She looked as if she had been ill, too.

"I have to know what has happened," I said.

"Yes." She pulled up a straight-backed chair. "Your parents were buried yesterday, Frue. I went to the funeral."

Buried . . . gone. And I had not been there. But they had "gone" all in a moment when the rocket hit the house beyond the mews. Their bodies still sitting there, their eyes open, but indisputably gone. In a strange flash

36

of knowledge, I was *glad* that I had been there and had seen them after the blast. I knew, as I sat on the edge of the bed, still staring at Aunt Mildred, that there was much that I had to think out as soon as my head was really clear. Where they had gone, if anywhere; what I believed. My parents were agnostics, and I had never been sent to church. And we were a varied bunch at the Lennox School. There were many like me, as well as Christians, Jews, and a few of Eastern religions.

On the whole, I thought, I don't think I shall ever believe other than that they have gone. Finished. All that life, all that loving and hope for the future. Aunt Mildred will say differently. She is religious. She goes to Great Hartsthorn Church. I remember her saying so, and Father said, after she had left, "The way to heaven is smoothed by arranging the flowers at the altar."

"They are with God, Frue, dear," said Aunt Mildred. Her voice shook a little; she had had a bad time and maybe she had been really fond of my mother, her niece. I opened my mouth to say something bitter and clever, but I never said it. I had looked down at my dressing gown and slippers.

"Why, they're my own!" I cried. "My own slippers!" Old, old blue slippers, the right one with a burned toe from putting it too near the fire to warm.

"Yes," she said. "A lot of things came yesterday. Mr. and Mrs. Tremartin packed everything up that could be rescued from the house and sent them by rail. I never had much opinion of artists, but they are really Christian people."

They were not, in her sense; they were atheists. But it was the same thing in this case. They were kind and thoughtful, and I was not so alone in the world as I had thought. Alone physically, but things did count.

"What came?" I asked, and she told me. "Several boxes and an old trunk. Books, clothes, and some of your mother's jewelery. Not worth much, I'm afraid, but you may like to have it. Most of the clothes were dusty. Muriel washed your dressing gown, and dried it by the kitchen fire. When you're better you can go through everything. It's all in the blue room. One thing about this house," she added wryly, "there's plenty of room."

"I am better," I told her, though my head was starting to ache.

"Not that much better. Come and wash your face."

I washed my face and it felt good. Then someone came stumping up the stairs, and an old woman appeared carrying a tray. There was the smell of soup.

"Miss Muriel heard voices. . . . Is the lassie better?"

"Yes, Katie, she's getting better. She'll get back into bed and have the soup. Frue, this is Katie Hobart, who lives with us and helps us."

"Hello!" I said. I had heard of Katie Hobart; I even remembered meeting her when I was nine. She had seemed about ninety then. She was a real Bucks woman. Her husband had been a bodger, following the ancient skill of making chair legs on a pole lathe in the beech-woods. And she had been skilled at making lace; the real, handmade Buckinghamshire lace.

Aunt Mildred settled me back in bed and I drank the soup. It was very good. Feeling stronger, I said, "Aunt Mildred, you are all being very kind to me, but I'm missing school and I had a small part in a West End play. Madame Ramier must be in a frightful state, and . . . the show must go on, you know. When can I go back to London? Madame would find me somewhere to live. They haven't a boardinghouse in London since the war, but . . ."

Aunt Mildred looked less kind and more like her old self, disapproving and dominating.

"You must forget all that, Frue. You can't go back to London. The rockets are still falling, and . . . well, this is your home now, as it should have been years ago. As for your Madame, she has been informed and understands. I believe the understudy has taken over your part in the play."

"But she can't . . . *you* can't . . .!" I knocked over the empty bowl and the tray slipped from the bed with a crash. "I can't stay here, Aunt Mildred. Something could be arranged." My mind began to work furiously, in a panic. "I must have some money, and it can be used . . ."

"You have very little money, Frue," Aunt Mildred told me, quite gently.

No money! Of course they had been talking about money on that fatal New Year's Eve. But that had been big money, for making films.

"Didn't my father leave anything?" I asked, and choked. I was hot all over and starting to shake again.

"You had better know the truth, once and for all," Aunt Mildred said. "The house was rented, and most of the furniture was destroyed. It's still early to be sure, but your father seems to have had only a few hundred pounds in a savings account, and thirty-six pounds in his checking account at the bank. No other assets. Typical of him, he didn't insure his life. You'll probably get

39

something from the Army, but in any case I couldn't think of allowing you to go back to London alone. You are my responsibility, and this is your home now."

She meant to be kind; she did mean to be. Maybe she really wanted me. But she would imprison me, as she had Muriel. Aunt Mildred ate people. She had always minded that my mother had married a man of whom she disapproved. The fact that she had not liked my father was enough to turn me against her. Father was a wonderful man, and there was never any doubt that he and Mother belonged together. But Aunt Mildred would never see it, and it was a point that I could not argue; I knew that.

I sank back on the pillows and, alone again, faced the unbelievable future. Right now I couldn't fight. I was stuck with Little Hartsthorn, that tiny village so remote from the war. Helpless in Aunt Mildred's hands, cut off from my old life. The understudy taking my place in the play. A nice girl, prettier than I, she would probably be secretly glad. Who *wouldn't* be glad?

I did not know then how to face my new life, but I knew I would have to, since I was still alive. Father had always said I was a person in my own right, and he had treated me as such. Aunt Mildred would somehow have to learn that I wasn't just a child, to be pushed around.

As I drifted into a doze, Mrs. Tremartin's voice echoed in my head: "Be kind to her." What an extraordinary thing to say. Aunt Mildred needed kindness just about as little as the back of a bus.

4

Buried in Beechwoods

The next day Muriel brought me some of my own clothes, neatly washed and ironed. Underclothes, my school skirt, and a blue sweater. I was better, I could have a bath (as little hot water as possible, according to wartime dictum), and get dressed.

I would much have preferred to stay in the gable room, with the comfort of the wood fire, but I obeyed because I hadn't the strength to argue. I had lunch in the big dining room with Aunt Mildred and Muriel. There was rabbit stew and apple pie, and I found that I was hungry. It was better food than I was used to most of the time in London. It seemed terrible, almost shameful, to be hungry, but I could not resist those delicious dishes. As old Katie cleared away the plates she said, "Anyone can see the lassie's better."

I was better in body, but not in spirit, and I hardly spoke at all. Aunt Mildred talked about the Red Cross, what the vicar had said, and how the hens were laying, and a lot of other trivial things. Her tone to Muriel was always slightly bullying, but Muriel didn't seem to notice. She had a remote air, and once I caught her smiling to herself. The smile made her look very attractive, in spite of the fact that she wore no makeup and her double-knit sweater was of a dreary brown-gray. She wore breeches, like a Land Girl, and though they were of some bulky material, she had quite a good figure.

I found myself vaguely interested in my cousin Muriel. It seemed awful that she had got imprisoned in Little Hartsthorn, and I wondered why she had not rebelled like her sister, Molly. I knew very little about Molly; only that she had had a tremendous row with her mother about fifteen years ago and had gone off to London, then to Paris. She had married soon after she left home and had a child; Mother had told me. That was all she knew. Apparently Molly had written once or twice, but—"Aunt Mildred isn't a very forgiving kind of person," Mother had said.

After lunch I was shown the blue room and told that I could look through the things that had come from London. Anything I wanted particularly, like books, could go in my room, and any of my own clothes that I could find.

It was bitterly cold in the blue room and Muriel brought a small electric heater. She asked if she could help, and I said no, so she went off to clean the hen house. I stood at the window for a time, looking out at the garden and the brooding woods. The dogs were down below, skirmishing together and barking. They were the only living things in the landscape. I was buried, it seemed, in beechwoods, which shut out the real world. On that first day, and for some days to come, I couldn't think of Little Hartsthorn as being allied in any way to reality.

But the old trunk and boxes were dreadfully real. In a way it was horrific to unpack them, but in another way

I was glad that they had come, because the things they contained were part of my old life. I certainly didn't want help and I stiffened as I heard voices arguing outside in the passage. Katie was saying it was wicked to leave me alone, and Aunt Mildred answered, "She has to face up to it, Katie, hard as it is. If she wants help she'll ask for it. Leave her alone."

The first good marks to Aunt Mildred. I would have thought she couldn't resist interfering.

Muriel had left dustcloths and I wiped my own books and carried them a few at a time to the gable room. They were damaged a little, but still readable. The dear books of my childhood, and some of my library of theatrical books. *Who's Who in the Theatre*, and volumes of plays.

Some of Father's film books were there, too, but they were more damaged than mine by dust and smoke. In another box there were all kinds of small things; one or two vases, actually unbroken, Mother's jewelery in a leather case, and her sewing basket. That last made my eyes burn with tears, as I remembered the green dress and my velvet skirt.

In the trunk, already opened by Muriel, there were piles of clothes, unfolded and mostly dusty. Seeing those was the worst thing. Prewar suits of Father's, Mother's skirts and dresses, all so shabby because the war had gone on for so long. And there were my own things, too, which I put in a pile to be washed. It was good to have my own clothes, and not to have to be fitted out by some wartime charitable organization.

At the very bottom was an old jacket that Father always wore when he came home on leave. He hadn't worn it at the party because Mother had said it was a disgrace. I pressed my face into it and, in spite of the dust, it still had his smell. There was a jingling sound and I found money in a pocket; four half crowns, three shillings, and several pennies. Almost guiltily I collected them and tried the other pocket. Crammed in there, rather crumpled, was a five pound note and two one pound notes. Treasure. Oh, Father! You never thought I would find the money in Little Hartsthorn, when you were dead.

I looked around the gable room for a safe hiding place, and decided on the depth of a fat Victorian vase on the mantelpiece for the loose change, wrapped in a handkerchief so that it wouldn't rattle, and one of my books, *Treasure Island,* for the notes. I might need that money one day to run away back to London.

Another thing I hid was Father's old jacket. I rolled it up and thrust it at the very back of the vast Victorian wardrobe in the gable room. I couldn't be sure why I wanted it so much, for a jacket is a jacket and not a person, but I *did* want it and I felt sure that Aunt Mildred wouldn't approve.

I had just finished, and was feeling very dusty and rather shaky, when Aunt Mildred appeared. She took in the scene in the blue room with one quick look and asked, "Got everything you want, have you? Then I'll ask the Women's Voluntary Service in Missencombe to pick up the rest of the clothes. Neither Muriel nor I are very good at sewing, so I doubt if we could alter any of your Mother's things for you. Besides, they look far too old."

I faced her, clasping my cold and dirty hands. "They

can't go to the WVS! Not my parents' things!" It seemed, somehow, the final outrage.

But she answered calmly, "They'll find a use for them, shabby as they are. Now wash your hands and come down to tea. You look tired. You aren't strong yet."

Strong. . . . I wanted to howl like a baby. I wanted to lie on the floor and kick my heels and scream. But I knew already that the only way to deal with Aunt Mildred was to keep my cool. That expression hadn't been invented then, but my upbringing had included the tacit assumption of self-discipline. Both my parents and the Lennox School believed in that rather than in imposed discipline. I had never really been put to the test before, certainly not to such a terrible test, but I did wash my hands and I walked quietly downstairs and drank weak tea out of a delicate china cup. My seeing eyes were still working overtime, and I still remember the exact shape and pattern of that cup. I remember the taste of the wartime scone, thinly daubed with margarine.

The vicar of Great Hartsthorn dropped in and gratefully accepted food and drink. Presumably he had come just then in the hope of them. He was a thin, rather elderly man called Browning, with blue-veined hands and shabby clerical clothes. He had a nice voice and was, to my surprise, not unctuous. I had never met a vicar before, and I had a rather "stage" picture of one, I expect. I shrank back into my chair, feeling sure he would immediately mention the death of my parents and drag in God's mercy or something.

He did neither. He said, "So you're Frue Allendale? I remember you when your father made the film *Traveler's*

Joy. You were only a little girl then, but very clever. We all went to see the film in Missencombe."

"*Did* you?"

"Everyone from the Hartsthorns went, I do believe, even your Aunt Mildred." And he shot a look that was distinctly amused at Aunt Mildred. Aunt Mildred said tartly, "Muriel wanted to go, and I suppose we all wanted to see what our local scene came out like. I couldn't make head or tail of the story, as you know, Vicar. Ghost children! I have my feet firmly on the ground."

After that they both ignored me, for which I was grateful, and it was only when he was leaving that the vicar touched me on the shoulder and said gently, "When you feel better come and see us at Great Hartsthorn vicarage. Muriel will lend you her bicycle, I expect. You'll have to push it uphill, but you'll spin back in no time."

And he went out into the dark-blue ice cold of the late afternoon, mounted his own shabby machine, and rode away. He had seemed nice enough, but I didn't think I'd go. The talk between him and Aunt Mildred had all been about polishing the brasses in the church, the next whist drive, and how good "Robert" was in seeing that they all got loads of wood from the estate. Whoever Robert was, he seemed uppermost in their talk. He sounded like a local farmer. I couldn't do that kind of talk and I wasn't going to try. With the rockets still falling on London, and all the terrible realities of the war, I could only despise such absorption in tiny local matters.

Later I tried to say something about it to Muriel, when we were washing the dinner dishes together. It was

Katie's evening when she went to see an old friend down the lane. And Muriel answered, "Well, Frue, were *you* always talking about the war, and big things, in London?"

I stared at her, taken aback. Of course we weren't. We had laughed, and talked nonsense, and gone to see plays and listen to wonderful concerts. We had eaten horrible food, and laughed about that, and shrugged off many of the awful things, because there was nothing else to be done. "We can't agonize all the time," Mother had said, during one of the darkest periods of the war. "Let's go to the zoo." Or sometimes it had been a silly film, or to stand in a queue at Coty's or Yardley's because there was a rumor that they had had a consignment of talcum powder and soap.

"No-o," I admitted slowly. "Of course not. But it wasn't like this place, so far from everything important. We were in the thick of things, and we knew about the latest plays and books, and . . . London's *different*."

"You mustn't think that, because people talk about everyday things, they forget the war. In fact they are . . ."

"Muriel!" called Aunt Mildred. "Are you going to be all night? I want you to go through these accounts with me."

Muriel finished putting away the dishes in silence, and we had no more conversation that night.

I dreamed that night, a nightmare of smoke and fire and loss, and I awoke knowing it had all been true, and that the loss was real. I must have screamed aloud, for Muriel came to me, wearing old flannelette pajamas and with bare feet on the icy floors. She bent over me and took me in her arms, and her dark, shiny hair, which she wore quite long, swept my cheek. "Never mind, chicken! It will soon be morning. It's six o'clock. Shall I stay with you?"

"Yes, please," I whispered, and she climbed into bed with me, shivering, and held me until I slept again. My last thought was how warm and kind she was, in spite of being bullied by Aunt Mildred, and it seemed a pity that she had no one to love her. No children of her own, and not even an interesting wartime job. So why wasn't she miserable and sharp and ugly?

When I awoke at eight o'clock she had gone, and I lay thinking until Katie brought me a cup of tea, telling myself that I must snap out of it, do something. The first thing was to telephone Madame. There must be a public phone somewhere, and I had money, though I would need more small change for a call to London. I might have to hold the line while the secretary looked for Madame. She was pretty sure to be there at the Lennox even though term hadn't started. There would be auditions and new parents to see.

So I agreed readily when Aunt Mildred said that what I needed now was fresh air. "You get out and explore," she said. "It's quite a nice morning; a heavy frost in the night, but the sun's going to shine. Go and look at the village and walk through Hartsthornleaf Wood. The church is very interesting. Some Saxon work and the rest pure Norman. Mr. Browning takes services here occasionally. We have no vicar of our own here now. On Sunday you'll come with us to Great Hartsthorn Church."

"I don't go to church," I told her, and she said, "You

48

do here. I never heard of such a thing! Not go to church."

"Plenty of people don't and are just as good . . ." But she snorted and walked away.

I collected my hidden change, put on my school coat that had been brushed, and my strongest shoes. The air outside smelled good. The dogs came rushing after me, barking. I hated those dogs, always underfoot, and lying around during meals. I shouted to them to go back, and, to my surprise, they did, looking disappointed. No walks for them with me! Muriel had said there were cats in the barn. I must find them for comfort.

I turned left and soon came to the "village." There was a tiny green, and an inn called the Hartsthorn Arms, and about eight cottages, all built of brick and flint, with roofs of russet tiles. One of the cottages was the post office and store. At the side was a telephone box, privately tucked into a hazel hedge. I went into the post office to buy stamps, because I must write to the Tremartins and to my best friend at the Lennox, Kristina Manopolis. Also I would get some change.

There were two women looking at the goods and another gossiping with the woman behind the counter. I caught a few words before they all stopped talking, and the woman behind the counter said, "You're the girl from London? Mrs. Butler's niece?"

"Yes," I said, then asked for my stamps. It wasn't my turn, but I only wanted to get out again, away from staring eyes.

I took the stamps and change and put them in my purse, then walked out, while the bell on the door made a great noise. The telephone box was not within their view, thank goodness. I got through to the Lennox quite quickly and, incredible luck, Madame Ramier herself

49

answered. She sounded relieved and glad when she heard my voice, and I almost broke down. It was the first contact I had had with my old life since the awful thing happened.

"I'm here at a place called Little Hartsthorn, and a kind of prisoner," I told her, when I could speak steadily. "Oh, Madame, they say I won't have much money, but I *must* get back. Oh, help me!"

Madame was French, but she had been in England a long time. Her voice had little trace of accent. "My dear Frue, I know where you are. I came there when you were ill."

"You *came?*" It was hard to believe. Madame was a very important, busy person, and I could not imagine her at Little Hartsthorn, dealing with Aunt Mildred. "They never told me."

"I offered to find you somewhere to live, and give you a scholarship at the Lennox," Madame said. "Your aunt wouldn't even consider the suggestion, and I fear you'll have to make the best of things for the moment, Frue. She told me she plans to send you to school locally."

That such things could be talked of and arranged, or not arranged, without my knowledge made me choke with rage and despair. "I won't go to a local school! I know nothing about it. My parents always told me things and let me choose."

"Your aunt's old-fashioned, but she means well by you, child. So . . ."

"But I can't stay here buried in beechwoods!" I howled, in deep despair. Oh, I must be out of my mind to howl at Madame. I had always been in some awe of her.

To my surprise she laughed, a deep, rich chuckle. "I must admit there are a large number of trees. Country to us both, I fancy, is the London parks. Now listen to me, Frue . . ." I was frantically cramming in more money, there was a rattle and a click, and she went on, "Be a brave girl and try to learn something from this. It always helps an actress to have deep experiences. You have some talent and you'll develop more. It won't do any harm to be away from London for a time. There'll always be a place for you at the Lennox. But, meanwhile, get really well and strong in the country. London isn't a good place just now. I'll keep in touch . . ."

"Oh, Madame!" I was crying into the receiver. So much for self-discipline.

"Your aunt means it for the best. Don't hate her."

But I did hate Aunt Mildred. She was drawing me down into the enclosed life of Little Hartsthorn. I walked blindly away from the telephone and past the tiny, plain church, and into Hartsthornleaf Wood. The smooth gray trunks of the beeches rose all around, with the winter sunshine slanting through onto the bracken. The russet fronds were still touched with glittering frost. Everywhere was utterly silent. It was peaceful and beautiful, and gradually I began to feel soothed, even comforted. For Madame had spoken of me as an actress. She had held out some vague hope for the future. That future seemed far away; the immediate future was problematical. I could bear it in a dull kind of way, or I could learn something new. That seemed to be the gist of it.

5

The Meeting with Robert

On my return to Dogwood House I wanted to tackle Aunt Mildred about what she had done, deciding my future without consulting me, but I knew it was no good. She wouldn't yield to me, if she had withstood Madame.

So I wandered around outdoors and found hen houses and a sty where a pig was grunting and smelling very strong. There was a huge old barn with an arched entrance, almost like a church. I went slowly into its dimness and found a ladder leading to a loft. There was a small side window that gave me light enough to find apples stored in straw. I wiped one and ate it; it was crisp and sweet.

The roof of the barn looked very ancient, with huge wooden beams. At some time Dogwood House must have been a farm. The loft would be a good place to hide when I needed to be alone. The ladder wasn't easy to manage, and would probably be too much for Aunt Mildred.

When I climbed down I heard a mewing sound and found a beautiful tortoiseshell cat with four kittens in a nest of straw. Sunlight through the open door slanted on them, making their fur shine. Somehow a cat with growing kittens really was a comfort.

Muriel found me there. "Would you like to look for eggs?" she asked, and I said "No," baldly. Then, "No, thank you, Muriel."

"What's the matter?" she asked, looking down at me as I crouched on the floor of beaten earth. I rose and faced her.

"I telephoned Madame at the Lennox School. She told me she came . . . that Aunt Mildred wouldn't. . . . How do you *bear* living here? Why didn't you run away like your sister?"

Muriel was wearing the breeches and two immensely thick sweaters. I had seen her clearing sprout stalks in the kitchen garden as I slipped into the barn.

She might have been annoyed with me, but she answered quietly, after a pause. "It may surprise you to know, Frue, that I'm very fond of my mother. She isn't an easy person, but I understand her. These things happen. Molly was always a rebel and they never got on. I might have gone if my father hadn't died. But after that I couldn't . . . Mother was just broken by his death. They quarreled sometimes, but she adored him."

Broken? Adored? Aunt Mildred, who seemed so hard and cold. I just could not imagine her loving a man.

"He died of a heart attack when he was only fifty-three. That's twelve years ago. He was two years younger than Mother."

"But when the war came you had your chance. You could have joined one of the Services, but you let her stop you."

Muriel looked very grave. "Frue, you don't know anything about it. It wasn't like that. Look, I'll tell you, but you mustn't speak of it. Your mother never knew; hardly anyone was told. Mother wanted it that way. Early in the war she found she had cancer. It was a very bad time. She had an operation, but I felt I couldn't leave her. I was needed here, anyway, with all the evacuees."

I was appalled. Cancer . . . that dreaded word, hardly ever spoken. Aunt Mildred!

"But she's still alive."

"She was cured. At least, they said it might never recur. But that's why I stayed. And I like Little Hartsthorn. Believe me, I'm not unhappy, whatever you may have heard or thought. There are good and splendid people here, and we haven't been as far from the war as you may think. I love this countryside, and you'll learn to love it too."

"I'm a Londoner."

"Other Londoners came in the early days and stayed for some years. A few are here still. Can you ride a bicycle?"

"Yes. I never owned one, but I have ridden sometimes."

"Then borrow mine and go exploring for a few days. The cold won't harm you if you're well wrapped up. But come home before dark. I have maps. Can you read a map? It's a help, as there are no signposts." They had all been taken away years before, in case of a German invasion.

"I can read a map," I said. I had learned long ago, during those idyllic days in Cornwall. Father loved maps and had a collection of old London ones. They had not been in the boxes, I remembered. They had gone forever, along with so much else.

"You're cold," Muriel said. I was not really cold, but

desolation had settled on my heart again. I went into the house and crept up the stairs. Now that I was better there was no longer a wood fire in the gable room, but the sunshine was pouring in. Still wearing my coat, I began to write in my diary. It was some relief to get it all down in writing.

Aunt Mildred had been to Missencombe on the bus. There *was* a bus service of sorts, it seemed, run by a private company appropriately named Farmer. When she came back at lunchtime she looked so normally brisk that I could hardly believe Muriel's story.

She told me that I now had a new identity card, a ration book, and clothing coupons, after a good deal of red tape down at the Food Office and other places. My old ones had been buried somewhere in the ruins of our house, or someone had stolen them.

I said the first thing that came into my head. It was really just a way of pushing aside memories of that ruined house. "May I have my sweet coupons?" Yet I did want to have them. Sweets, even wartime ones, were a comfort. I couldn't fight Aunt Mildred, standing there in her worn tweed coat and unbecoming hat, and everything was awful. I might as well have some toffee.

Aunt Mildred looked startled, but she tore the page out of the book. She then took two half crowns out of her purse and handed money and coupons to me. "Children need sugar. This is two weeks' pocket money." After a pause, she added, "I suggest you save some of it."

I promptly felt guilty about my hidden hoard. Half a crown a week was quite generous. I had not really expected anything. But money meant freedom. Young people are so helpless because they have no money. I had earned some a few months ago, when I acted in the West End, but it had all been used for some very special ballet lessons with a woman who had been a great dancer. I never wanted to go in for ballet, but a good knowledge of it would be a help to an actress. The little part I had just lost had included a short dance.

After lunch, with admonitions from Aunt Mildred to be careful coming downhill on the narrow lanes, I took Muriel's bicycle and rode out of the village toward Hartsthorn Bottom. When I reached the other road I turned away from Missencombe, heading for the hills, but soon stopped. For I had come to something that struck a chord of remembrance. At the side of the road were great wrought-iron gates leading, not to a conventional driveway, but to a broad stretch of green grass going smoothly uphill. And far away, dominating the rise, was a great house. The cold sunlight lay slantwise across its long frontage, which was covered with creeper.

Memory . . . I knew that house. I was looking at the East Front, which was later than most of it. Dimly I remembered a row of Adams drawing rooms. As a child of nine I had been allowed to peep into each one, and we had filmed a sequence of *Traveler's Joy* in the great Tudor banqueting hall.

I propped up the bicycle and stared through the gates, remembering. I hadn't thought of it for years, but I had been Joy in that house. I had leaned, as the ghost child, on the gallery railings, looking down at the portrait of Queen Elizabeth the First on the paneled wall, and the other portrait of Robert Speen, once owner of the house, who had been a friend of John Hampden, and who, like

57

him, had died in the Civil War. The smell of the house was suddenly all around me; a smell of early spring flowers, old wood, and—possibly—mice. I was always susceptible to smells. That house had been romance to me. It had been there, it was said, six hundred years before the first Elizabeth paid it a long visit. The green rise up which I was gazing was called Hartsthorn Stretch, and legend said it had been cleared overnight so that the great queen could have a view of the surrounding countryside. Just like the Glade at Hampden, another wonderful house that could not be far away.

I took out Muriel's map and, yes, I was right. That was Hartsthorn House, the seat of the Earl of Hartsthorn. The earl and countess had been away while we were working, but there had been a butler, very dignified, to see that "the film people" did not overstep the mark. We were lucky to have gained permission to make part of the picture there. Frobisher, that butler had been called. It was he who had taken me to peep into the drawing rooms, and he had also shown me a twisting stone staircase going down, strangely, from one of the bathrooms.

"This is King Henry's Tower, miss," he had said. I never knew which Henry, but an early one. There was a tiny garden called King Henry's Garden, close to the tower. Joy had been filmed wandering between the low box hedges.

And there it still was, splendidly topping the rise, while Joy, and the child I had been, had long gone. Untouched by the war, dreaming and stately, the great house cast a spell on me. Vaguely I resented it, because it seemed so remote from everything that had happened during the long years of deprivation and horrors; yet I was glad it was still there. More than St. Paul's Cathedral, most people's symbol of the heart and spirit of England, that vast house, rooted in long history, seemed to promise that we would win the war and know peace again.

Peace . . . when it came I could only be sad, because my parents had gone, and I had no one in the world but Aunt Mildred and Muriel. There was Madame, of course; I did believe she would not forget me, and the Tremartins. Paul had said he would think of something.

I forgot the house and, clinging to the gate with cold hands encased in very worn gloves, I suddenly longed for that tall figure; the boy who had kissed me on New Year's Eve. If I were never to see him again . . . but I couldn't face that thought. Out of all that had happened on that fatal New Year's Eve, those minutes in the kitchen alone with Paul Tremartin came back as a warm, real thing. Maybe he *would* think of something. Paul seemed to me steady and basically kind.

Slowly I pushed the bicycle uphill. At one point the road swung around and bisected the Stretch. Either way the green grass lay in pale sunshine. Looking up, the house was much nearer. The road passed through trees, and seeded willow herb shimmered silver in the cold shadows. Then I was up the hill and I came to a white gate, wide open, and the real driveway of Hartsthorn House, with a pretty lodge at the side.

CHURCH AND FOOTPATH ONLY, said a small sign, pointing up the drive, which was bordered with splendid old beech trees. Church . . . it was close to the house. Vaguely

I remembered it, and the Speen family tombs. The Sir Robert Speen who had died on Chalgrove Field was buried there.

Away, away rolled the winter fields and the russet-purple woods. I had seen no car, not one person, since I left Hartsthorn Bottom. And suddenly I was very cold, and lonely, and wanted to be indoors. At three o'clock the day was already dying.

I mounted and rode back downhill. The icy wind whistled past my face, though my head and ears were protected by an old woolen helmet of Muriel's. Silver and shadow; sunlight still on the chalky fields. If this was to be my new world it was a very beautiful one; I was in no doubt of that. But in January, in my present mood, it was a sad one. What did people *do* in the country? Well, they farmed. As I swooped over the Stretch I saw a horse-drawn plow turning up the pale earth in a distant field, and, even so far from the sea, sea gulls were flying behind it in a white cloud.

The blacksmith was working at Hartsthorn Bottom. I paused to look into the forge, where he was shoeing a great carthorse. There was warmth and a strange smell.

I whizzed along the winding lane to Little Hartsthorn. On the right, before Dogwood House, there was a large farm. A big house built of brick and flint, and many buildings. Hay and straw stacks gleamed in the last of the sunlight. The haystacks were round, an odd shape. I was looking at them and not worrying about the possibility of traffic in the lane. I swung around the next corner, and then I shrieked, and braked, and tumbled off the bicycle almost under the nose of a horse.

I landed rather hard and, worst of all, in a large cowpat. Hands hauled me up and a nice voice asked if I was all right.

"I'm fine," I said confusedly. "I'm sorry. I was looking at the haystacks. I didn't know they were round. I'm going to smell awful."

He laughed. He was a farmer, wearing a thick jacket, dirty trousers, and mud-caked boots. Dark haired, not good looking, with a thin, pleasant face. For a moment I felt I had seen him before. The cart he had been driving was laden with turnips or something.

"Haystacks *are* round in Buckinghamshire," he said. "You must be the little girl from Dogwood House. Frue Allendale?"

"Yes. But I'm fifteen; not little." I was conscious of a terrific smell of cow. "I'm sorry I nearly rode into your horse. I'm not used to the country, I thought there was no traffic."

"There isn't much. Hardly anyone has petrol," he said. He looked amused. "I don't know what Mildred will say when she sees you. I'd try to find Muriel first. She'll deal with you."

"Thanks." I picked up the bicycle, which seemed undamaged, and pushed it past the cart. He climbed up again and drove on. I looked back to see him turning into the big farm. Suddenly Muriel was at my elbow. Unnoticed, she had come along the lane from Dogwood House.

"I'm afraid I stink," I said, but it was all too evident. "Don't tell Aunt Mildred I nearly knocked down a horse. I was all right otherwise, really. That man said you'd be the best one to see first, so it's lucky . . ."

"Very lucky." She was laughing. Her face, usually

61

with a rather remote expression, seemed wholly alive. "Robert knew who you were, did he?"

"Robert? Oh, is *that* Robert? The one who lets you have the wood? I've heard him mentioned several times. They were even talking about him in the village shop when I went in to buy stamps this morning."

"That's Robert," she said. "He lives at Little Harts-thorn Farm. Didn't you know, Frue? He's the Earl of Hartsthorn."

6

My Cousin Muriel

I stood stock still in the lane, blank with astonishment. The air, now really icy, held great clouds of my breath as I gasped, started to speak, stopped again.

"That man . . . that farmer . . . he *can't* be the earl!" I finally got out. "Why, the earl must be quite old. The butler showed me a portrait of him when we filmed at Hartsthorn House." In the picture he had been a man in late middle age, with a thin face, a long nose, and very elegant hands. It was strange how clearly I suddenly saw that portrait over the gap of the years. I heard the butler's precise voice saying, "The master is the fourth earl, miss."

"He is the earl, all the same," Muriel said. "The fifth Earl of Hartsthorn. His parents were killed in a car accident three days after war was declared in 1939. It was a terrible tragedy. Robert lived in the house for a few months, but the war and the death duties made it impossible. Most of the staff had left. The butler you remember retired; the head housemaid joined the Wrens and took two underhousemaids with her. The cook has spent the war working in an armed forces canteen. The old order has gone, as in so many other places, Frue. Robert lives at Little Hartsthorn Farm, looked after by an old woman who used to be his nanny. And Hartsthorn House is let on a long lease. It's a school."

"A *school?*" And I had thought that great house had been left untouched, dreaming there on the ridge.

"A boarding school for older girls. It moved from Hampstead in the spring of 1940."

"So is the earl *poor?*" I asked, and she laughed and answered, "Oh, no, not by our standards. He gets an income from the estate, which is a very large one, with several hamlets and farms, and hundreds of acres of fine timber. The estate is in trust for his son, if he ever marries and has one." Her voice was cool, noncommittal, and her own breath surged up in clouds against the dying light. "If not, it goes, with the title, to a distant cousin." Then she asked, with a quick change of tone, "You said they were talking about him in the village shop. How do you mean?"

At the time I had taken little notice, though the faces of the women had impinged themselves on my mind because of my new powers of observance. They had all been "cottage women" pretty certainly. One had worn an apron under her coat, and one had had her hair in curlers.

"One was saying something about Robert going to London all dressed up far more than he used to," I repeated glibly. "And the other said, 'Ah, but there must be an attraction there.' The woman behind the counter frowned at them and looked at me. And she muttered something about 'not suitable to call him Robert.' I was buying stamps, and they were all staring at me, so I came out quickly."

"It isn't suitable, but they all do it behind his back,"

Muriel said, in a tone that was suddenly sharp. "They've known him since he was born, of course. His grandmother used to take soup to the old people on the estate, in the manner of the very old days, and Robert had to go with her when he was little. He's often said how he hated it, and always wondered why the old lady didn't get the soup thrown in her face. She was very arrogant and enjoyed being the lady of the manor. That was nearly thirty years ago, of course, but things were already changing. Though some almost feudal things survived. There was always a Christmas party in the Tudor banqueting hall for the children of the estate right up to the war, and actually Mrs. Hailey-Reed carries it on. She's the head of the school. The girls entertain the children, and there's a huge Christmas tree, and presents, and a fire of yule logs from the estate. The only time a fire is ever lit in the great fireplace. *I* went to the party as a child." Her voice was still a little sharp, and I had the feeling she hadn't been pleased by the words I had repeated.

"But *you* weren't a cottage child." I had almost forgotten the cold, and my earlier misery, and the pungent smell of cow. But she seized me by the arm and hurried me up the drive toward the back door of Dogwood House.

"Got to get you to Katie before Mother comes in! She's gone out for a time. She wouldn't mind the mess you're in, but she might think you're unsafe on a bicycle. No, of course I wasn't a cottage child. We had plenty of money in those days. But we all went to the party. It had a kind of enchantment. If you remember the banqueting hall you'll be able to picture it. Robert hated that, too. He had to give out the presents when he was just a little boy and very shy. He stammered when he was young."

We were at the kitchen door. I said, "I suppose you remember the old lady, and the soup, and everything? You're older than Robert. I mean the earl."

"Five years." She flung open the door and gave me a jerk, so that I almost fell into the scullery. In the light of a dim bulb I saw that she looked a bit grim, and I couldn't think how I had upset her that time. It was all very interesting; quite the stuff of a play or a novel. For the very first time I had forgotten my sorrow, and my hatred of being there in that hamlet among the hills.

"Frue fell in some cow muck," Muriel said brusquely to Katie, who was sitting by a roaring wood fire. The kettle was singing on the hob, and a tray loaded with plates of bread and margarine, homemade blackberry jam, and plain cake stood ready on the table. I promptly felt hungry, for the jam, though not very sweet, was delicious.

"My God, don't let the mistress see her!" the old woman cried, and put a cloth over the tray of food. "She smells worse than the barley field did before Christmas. Get back into the scullery, my dear, and take off your coat and shoes. Your good coat, too. It'll have to be washed, and that won't improve it. Unless we can smuggle it down to the cleaners in Missencombe. Then what'd you wear while it's away?"

"I have another one," I said. For my old brown coat had been in the trunk; short, and with a hole in the elbow, but wearable. I felt about seven as the old woman bustled around me, and also incredibly foolish. If I *had* to fall off my bike, why into a cowpat? Yet it was a bit funny. I gave a faint giggle. The hazards of living in the country.

Aunt Mildred came in ten minutes later, but by then I was washed and brushed and in different stockings. Muriel and I were in the sitting room and we began tea at once. Aunt Mildred glanced at me critically and said, "You look better, Frue. Quite a color. How far did you go?"

"To the gate of Hartsthorn House," I told her, and Muriel said, "She met Robert in the lane coming back."

"Robert . . ." Aunt Mildred's face softened. "We must ask him to dinner one night when we have something decent to eat. It's about time the pig was killed. Make arrangements, Muriel, will you?"

"Not killed here?" I asked, choking on a piece of bread and jam.

She gave me a scornful look. "Why not? You mustn't be a little softy, Frue. You'll enjoy roast pork like the rest of us. But don't chatter about it. There are regulations. Those theatrical people in London don't know they're born, with that unnatural life. We'll show you something different, and more earthy, here. You'll soon get over being squeamish. If we get a softer spell of weather, the kitchen garden needs digging over. You can help. Robert sent a cartload of manure."

Oh, no more manure! Even Katie's wartime cake (which was better than most) failed to tempt me after that. I thought I would ask for some writing paper and write to the Tremartins and Kristina that evening. I would make a good tale of my adventures to the Tremartins if it killed me. But I would make it clear how desperately I wanted to be rescued from Aunt Mildred.

Several days passed. Every night I had the same recurring nightmare, but evidently I never cried out again, for Muriel did not come to me. She had been warm and almost motherly that night, but since then she had seemed remote. I had the feeling that much was going on in her mind, but that she was in the habit of keeping all her thoughts to herself.

There was tension between me and Aunt Mildred. I resented her manner to me, and hated her because she had refused Madame's offer. Also I couldn't help looking at her with a kind of horror, because of the cancer that might not be dead. I didn't know how she could go on seeming so normal, with that danger inside her.

I should have admired her. I did, in a way, but we seemed to meet nowhere. It was to be expected, of course, because Father had never thought her our kind of person.

She was quite kind to me, in a brisk, critical way, but the desolation in my heart increased as the days passed. I would sooner have read, written in my diary, and dreamed than be pushed into various activities, most of them uncongenial. But she wouldn't leave me alone. I must get out . . . work in the garden . . . feed the hens . . . explore the countryside. The fact that the weather was so cold seemed not to trouble her. She was out in all weathers; walking up to Great Hartsthorn or Hartsthorn Common on various missions, taking the bus into Missencombe. The telephone rang often and it was always something to do with the Women's Institute, the Red Cross, or the church. She seemed to run the whole area.

If I stayed in my room she rooted me out. "Come on,

Frue! Don't stuff indoors. I want a message taken to . . ."

Sometimes I took refuge in the kitchen with Katie. I liked Katie and her stories of the old days, when she had lived in a cottage at Hartsthorn Common and her husband had been a bodger in Great Hartsthorn Wood. She told me where there were bodgers still, up near Hartsthorn End, and I went to find them. It was a dying trade, turning those chair legs on a pole lathe, for the furniture factory down in Missencombe. There was a soothing fascination in watching the shavings fly.

Katie had a radio in the kitchen and I listened wistfully to news of London, though it was often bad. Still rockets falling. But Katie liked light music and that made me unbearably sad. Vera Lynn singing "There'll be blue birds over the white cliffs of Dover" was a knife in my heart, because my parents would not be there when peace came. I only liked orchestral and ballet music, anyway. I thought Vera Lynn was pretty feeble, though she was immensely popular; the Forces' sweetheart, she was called.

On Sunday morning we went to church at Great Hartsthorn, and Robert, Lord Speen, the fifth Earl of Hartsthorn, took us in his car. He had a petrol allowance because of being a farmer and managing the estate. He looked different then, very proper in a shabby town suit. He wasn't good looking, but he had a nice face; not a strong face, but kind. I didn't know what to call him. My Lord? But when I stammered awkwardly he laughed and said, "Oh, call me Robert as the others do, Frue."

The church was close to the great house, as I remembered, and it was rather beautiful in a dim, sad way.

69

There were not many people at the service, for gone were the days when the whole household and people of the estate attended as a matter of course. Robert read the first lesson and his voice was lovely. He might have made a good actor, I thought. He certainly didn't stammer now.

But I hated the service, which meant very little to me. "Oh, Lord, we have erred and strayed like lost sheep." More of that country idea. And the hymns made me want to cry, they were so dismal. "The King of Love my Shepherd is . . ."; another rural theme. I was glad to get out into the cold air and see the south side of the great house, with King Henry's ancient tower and the thick old hedge that hid King Henry's Garden. It seemed a million years since Joy had walked in that garden with cameras trained on her.

The next evening Robert came to dinner. The pig had not yet been killed so there was roast chicken, and a pudding made from bottled blackberries. Muriel had mended my velvet skirt very badly, but, in any case, I wouldn't have worn it or my royal-blue blouse. I felt I could never bear to wear those clothes again, even though I had so little choice. It was less than two weeks since that fatal night, and the memory grew more painful rather than less.

I wore an old blue dress that was too short and very shabby, and I was silent most of the time. Aunt Mildred and Robert talked about the estate, and the people on it, and I learned some things that I had not known. That the vicar had lost all three of his sons in the war; two in the Battle of Britain and one at Arnheim. And that the woman who kept the store and post office, Mrs. Baird, had lost her only son on D Day and a daughter who had been a nurse in a London hospital that was bombed. It was a shock, somehow, though I ought to have known that the war was no respecter of persons. I still felt that the Hartsthorns were incredibly remote from all that counted.

Another shock was when Robert spoke of the House of Lords. I knew very little about politics. My father hadn't been interested, though he was vaguely Socialistic, and so, I knew, were the Tremartins. I couldn't imagine Robert in all the ceremony of the House of Lords, though apparently he went up to London a few times a year to take part in special debates or when an important Bill came up. He knew Winston Churchill, and spoke of him familiarly as "Winston" . . . another shock. He had even stayed at Blenheim Palace and other great, important houses and castles. It was fascinating, in a way, but I had trouble keeping fully awake. I'd never have felt sleepy if the talk had been about the theatre.

Muriel was nearly as quiet as I was. She wore a pink sweater and a gray skirt and looked much tidier than usual. She had nice legs, I discovered, and quite elegant feet now that I saw them out of boots or old slippers. Once I saw her exchange looks with Robert when Aunt Mildred was giving an order to Katie. Of course they really knew each other quite well. In a way they had grown up together.

When we had finished coffee Robert said he must go, as he was expecting a sow to farrow and it might be a difficult birth. Aunt Mildred saw him off, and when she came back she said, "He's a nice man, but not forceful enough. Time he was married. I never listen to gossip,

71

but I hear he's been going up to London more often than usual. Maybe there's a strong, healthy girl there. Best thing for him."

Her eyes passed over me and rested on Muriel, who was starting to clear away coffee cups. "Pity Muriel is so much older than he is. I once had hopes of Molly, but she and Robert didn't get on when they were young, and then she went away. Throwing away a good chance of being a countess."

Her tone was casual, really; maybe not intentionally cruel, but I saw Muriel's shoulders stiffen. It must be *awful* to have it pointed out that you are not as young as you were, and five years older than the only eligible man in the village, and he an earl.

"Anyway," Aunt Mildred went on, "you're not the marrying kind, are you, Muriel? Thank goodness it's too late now. I couldn't do without you."

It was like a play; a really emotional one. Muriel's eyes seemed to grow darker, and her face was stiff with anger, or pain.

"You may remember, Mother," she said, "that I was very much the marrying kind, but *you* made sure that it came to nothing. I thought I'd forgiven you long ago, but there's no need to fling it in my face." And she went out, banging the door violently behind her.

I was riveted, quite forgetting myself and my own troubles. Really much more had gone on in the Harts-thorns than I had thought. I had found Muriel a great puzzle from the start, and now here she was with a lost romance, abandoning her habitual calm for a fury of temper and remembered sorrow.

Aunt Mildred piled up the remaining dishes on the tray.

"You get off to bed, Frue," she said sharply to me. Then, apparently talking to herself, "I'd almost forgotten, and I thought she had. He was quite unsuitable; some young man she met in London. She used to go up to town quite often in those days, and belonged to several clubs. He was a struggling musician, only half English. His mother was Polish or something. Franz Karl Delaney was his name, and he was a Roman Catholic to boot. Cecil said I was wrong, but he was always silly about Muriel. The only times we quarreled, it was over the girls. He was easy going and I demanded high standards from them both. If Molly had stayed and married Robert . . . but she went off and married some nobody, and . . ."

I had not gone to bed. I was still standing by the dying wood fire.

"Franz Karl Delaney," I repeated slowly. "But he's a famous pianist. I went to a concert he gave in St. Martin's-in-the-Fields before Christmas." A wonderful concert, as most of the wartime ones were; Chopin in the famous church on Trafalgar Square.

Aunt Mildred knocked a coffee cup off the tray and it broke. She bent to pick up the pieces. "This set is irreplaceable. I'd forgotten you were there, Frue. Yes, he achieved his aim. I've heard him on the radio. But it was only after years of struggle. I didn't want any daughter of mine to starve in a garret, though Molly may have done for all I know. *Go* to bed, Frue."

I went slowly upstairs. I was quite willing to starve in

a garret if I could go on trying to be an actress, and maybe Muriel would have done it for love.

Muriel's bedroom door was closed and I could hear no sound within the room. Softly I tried the door and it opened. Muriel was standing by the bed; she looked restless and feverish.

"Go away, Frue!"

"But . . ."

"Mother doesn't believe in keys in doors," she said bitterly. "Is there *no* privacy in this house?"

"*You* tried to comfort me," I said uncertainly. I was a little afraid of her.

"I don't need comfort. It was all long ago, before you were born."

"But . . . Aunt Mildred was kind of talking to herself. She said it was Franz Karl Delaney, and I heard him play only just before Christmas. What did she *do?* How could she stop you? Do you . . . still love him?"

"Don't talk like a novelette," she said curtly. "We're not in a play now." Muddled, but I understood that she had some grasp of the fact that I thought in terms of the theatre and films. But I did like her, and she had been kind to me. I wished I were older and wiser.

"Once and for all," said my cousin Muriel, "get no romantic ideas on that score. People don't normally go on loving over many years, Frue, for no reason at all. My mother wrote Franz the most unforgivable letter. She showed me a copy of it. And he didn't make any fight. He went off to Warsaw and I never heard from him again. He's married with five children, I believe. Does that satisfy you?"

Before I was born was a long time ago, and her tone

74

was convincing. It all seemed very sad and terrible, that a mother could behave like that. *My* mother was all warmest love, and gaiety and openheartedness, and she had gone forever, leaving me in this house in the remote Chilterns.

"You hate her," I said. "And you told me you were fond of her."

"I *am* fond of her. Things are rarely clear cut, Frue. She can't help being the way she is. It was just that reference; the way she spoke. I . . . I was feeling a bit tense, anyway."

I let that pass. I didn't quite see why she should have been tense. It had been a pleasant dinner party, if rather dull.

"But . . . it's left you not loving anyone. And now it's too late."

Muriel seized me by the shoulders and swung me toward the door. "Go to bed, Frue. I'm not used to conversations like this. Love . . . the very young think it stops at thirty, even twenty. People have loved at sixty, seventy. When you learn that you'll have grown up a little. Love doesn't stop because people are older or old."

I was facing out, with her behind me. I heard myself saying an incredible thing. I wouldn't have thought I could, to an adult; to anyone.

"Sex stops, though."

"Who said?" snapped my cousin Muriel, and pushed me out and shut the door.

7

A Visitor from London

I collected my towel and went slowly into the ice-cold bathroom. The wind was howling around the house and something was beating softly against the window. It sounded like snow; too delicate for rain. Shivering, beset with new thoughts, I washed my face and hands and cleaned my teeth.

Baths were twice a week at Dogwood House. There was never much hot water, and you weren't supposed to use it, anyway. I could remember a time when I used to lie in the bath covered with deliciously scented water. That was before all the dreadful slogans that stopped you from enjoying yourself. Not only were you supposed to bath in about two inches of tepid water, but you were asked if your journey was really necessary, and suffered frightful guilt if you took a little holiday, like the time Mother and I went to Lincoln for a few days, or when Father, home on leave, fancied a trip to the Shakespeare Memorial Theatre at Stratford-upon-Avon. Another slogan was "Careless talk costs lives." The enemy, in some guise, might be listening if you talked about bombs in public. But that one didn't matter so much now that the Germans were almost beaten.

The war . . . people and their intricate problems . . . me

alone. Pushed out by Muriel with that astonishing question. Who *said?* No one said. I really had known that my parents were still in love, and it seemed strange, but they had been together for a long time and maybe it was habit. Basically I assumed that people had little feeling after they were, say, thirty. But there was feeling in Dogwood House.

My gable room was incredibly cold; the lovely wood fire that spluttered and then glowed was an unlikely dream. I scrabbled off my clothes, dived frantically into my pajamas, and dashed into bed, where Katie had put a blessed hot water bottle.

That night, instead of having a nightmare, I dreamed of Paul, but in a way it was nearly as bad, because when I woke up at four in the morning I realized that he might forget me and his promise.

At that hour I felt desperately miserable and lonely, and the hot water bottle was cold and no comfort. My new life included no one young. For the first time that really hit me. I had always been used to the varied company at the Lennox, and even in the holidays I still saw some of them. Kristina lived just the other side of the King's Road, and others not far away. And there was always the thought of the new term. Term . . . I would be sent to some other school. Locally, Madame had said. It must mean the high school down in Missencombe, but Aunt Mildred had told me nothing.

There were plenty of blankets on my bed, but I was cold, so cold. At last I fell asleep again, and again I dreamed of Paul. Someone young, someone who had kissed me. But he was in London and had forgotten me already.

When I got up there was a dusting of snow over the countryside, but the sun was shining. About eleven o'clock I walked into the village to see if Mrs. Baird had any toffee. Just as I reached the post office the old brown Farmer's bus from Missencombe swept along the lane and drew up beside the patch of snowy grass opposite the shop. I paused to watch it, noticing that a few passengers were getting off. When it moved away, to turn around, I saw two or three village women walking away, and one tall figure in a fawn duffle coat staring around him. He looked as if he had landed on the moon and didn't know what to make of it.

It was Paul Tremartin.

My heart did a great leap and I was convinced it was some illusion, some mirage. I looked at the brick-and-flint cottages, the little church in its tidy graveyard, and the great beech trees of Hartsthornleaf Wood encroaching to the west. The thin sunlight touched russet tiles and branches, lightly snow tipped. Everything sparkled in the icy air. Yes, a mirage . . . it must be.

I looked again, straight across the road, and he was still there, and now he was smiling. I didn't rush toward him. We both walked forward very slowly, and somehow now I can stand aside and see us both, quietly approaching, like two figures in a ballet. At the time, I only thought wildly that I must look awful, in Muriel's old woolen helmet and my shabby, too short brown coat. I wore rubber boots that I had never bothered to clean. They were thick with mud.

79

Slowly, slowly, until we were almost nose to nose in the middle of the road. And then, with a warning hoot, the bus bore down on us, having turned around up by the wood. There was a row of village women with market baskets waiting at the stop by the old, unused pump. Several of them shouted a warning, and Paul's hand shot out and dragged me onto the grass.

The bus driver leaned out and shouted, "Kiss your girl in a safer place, mate!" and Paul went very red. We stood there, never having said a word, until the bus had gone charging down the narrow lane. Then, suddenly, we both laughed and kept on laughing, rather hysterically.

"I couldn't believe it was you," I said, when I had recovered a little.

"And I never thought I'd have the luck to meet you like this," Paul confessed. "I thought I'd have to go up to the house and face your Aunt Mildred."

"But have you come all this way to see *me?*" Paul, who had almost always been aloof until New Year's Eve; so important at his famous London school and soon to go to Oxford. Not that he looked important, I thought. His thin face peered out from under the hood of his dreadful old duffle coat. Now that the blush had died he was very pale, almost gray; he didn't look well.

He began to talk quickly and nervously. "Well, you see, we got your letter and you sounded so unhappy, though you made a good tale of it. And Father said . . . Mother said . . . I thought . . ."

We were in full sight of the shop and post office, and Mrs. Baird was staring across interestedly. The whole village, the whole valley, maybe all the Hartsthorns, would know in a few hours that a young man had come

80

to see Frue Allendale. Suddenly I felt quite old and confident, and burning with a strange feeling I hardly recognized as happiness. I, who had thought I would never be happy again, even for one moment.

"Let's walk in the wood," I suggested. "Oh, Paul, I'm so glad to see you. You're the first young person I've talked to since . . . since I left London."

"Any hope of a cup of coffee?" he asked, glancing around. His gaze lighted on the inn, opposite the church, near the entrance to the wood.

"Oh, why, yes. At the inn," I said, in relief. "I know they do coffee, and Mrs. Clare might make us some sandwiches."

We walked together toward the inn, and Paul went first into the rather musty little parlor. A wood fire, newly lighted, was struggling for life. The place had only just opened, and no one was in the saloon bar, where the locals drank beer and played darts.

Backstage, as it were, Vera Lynn was once more singing, "There'll be blue birds over. . . ." I didn't mind it as much as usual.

Mrs. Clare looked in and her face showed open surprise. Me in the pub when I was under age, but only for coffee, after all.

"Why, Frue!" she cried. We had met in the village shop, and, besides, everyone knew me. You could hardly blow your nose in the Hartsthorns without causing interest. To remain anonymous for half a day, even, was impossible.

"Could we have some coffee, please, Mrs. Clare? And some sandwiches or something. My friend from London is hungry."

"London! Poor young man!" she said, eyeing Paul avidly. "Had a bad night in parts, I heard on the radio. Several of those nasty rockets. Still, it won't go on much longer. We've almost got them beat. Egg sandwiches are the best I can do, with a scraping of margarine."

As she went away someone on the unseen radio began to sing:

> "It's a lovely day tomorrow,
> Tomorrow is a lovely day . . ."

And I remembered that dreadful morning, two weeks ago, when I had heard that tune as I stood outside the Regent Palace Hotel.

"What's the matter, Frue?" Paul asked, and I said, "That song . . . a street musician was playing it when we stood outside the Regent Palace. Today isn't so bad now you're here, but tomorrow can't be a lovely day. None of my tomorrows can be lovely." Oh, dear! That was the worst of being an actress. I meant it with all my heart, but it sounded phony, somehow.

Paul began to tell me the news, rather quickly. That their house and the studio had really been quite badly damaged, but they hoped to get the place patched up in a few months. Meanwhile, they were sharing part of a house in Pimlico. It was very uncomfortable and crowded, and his father was going frantic because he had nowhere to paint.

"You're really better here, Frue," he told me. "London is pretty grim. Awful weather, and hardly any coal, and everyone seems to have got rather low. The war will end in the spring, everyone seems to think, but meanwhile..."
He swung around to look straight at me, and suddenly his face looked much better and brighter.

"Over. Finished. Think of it! Can you imagine it? There may be awful shortages for years in Britain, but we can get off the island; not imprisoned any more. By *next* spring I may have a passport and be able to go to Italy. Greece someday, even the Middle East. I'll be short of money as a student, but I'll go somehow. And, when I get there, all this winter horror and near hunger and boredom (for a lot of it *is* plain boring) will be unimportant. If I have to hitchhike, or *walk*, I'll get to some of the places I've dreamed about. I have to; I need to. It's to be my work."

I thought of all those countries I had never seen but had heard so much about throughout the war, and all of it terrible.

"It's a good thing you're interested in *ruins*," I said. "For I believe that's all you'll find."

"Yes," he agreed. "Think of landing in France off an *ordinary* Channel steamer. They will run again, but Calais will be gone. Razed to the ground. And all those cities . . . German cities, Frue, that were so beautiful. The year before the war we were in Dresden and a lot of other places. Father said we had to see them before it was too late. I was only a kid, but I remember. But the ancient sites will still be there in Italy and Greece, and some day I'll see them and maybe work in them."

Mrs. Clare brought the coffee and sandwiches, and he ate ravenously. "Sorry, only had plain toast for breakfast. Used up our rations. These are good."

I had had two eggs and lots of homemade jam, but I would have gone hungry if I could have been back in London.

Afterward we walked in Hartsthornleaf Wood. It was utterly silent, except for the sound of our feet on the

83

path. The gray trunks of the beeches loomed on either side, and there were holly bushes here and there, some still holding scarlet berries. The slanting light made the dark leaves gleam. The wood went on and on, touched by winter sunlight, snow on the russet bracken, and, while we walked, it was my turn to talk. I never thought I would talk so easily to Paul.

I told him everything, pouring it out. Aunt Mildred . . . Muriel . . . the earl . . . how I hated being in the country, and how I resented the fact that Aunt Mildred had refused to listen to Madame and her offer of a scholarship at the Lennox. I made scathing comments about country life, and sometimes he laughed, but by the end he was holding my hand.

"Oh, poor Frue! Everything must seem hopeless, I know. But you may grow to like this country. The hills and woods are beautiful, even in the depth of winter. It's very *ancient* country . . . I believe there are burial mounds and traces of Iron Age villages and other settlements. I wish we had time to look for some of them."

"Oh!" It had somehow never occurred to me that he didn't have to go to Greece or Italy to find ancient sites, though of course I knew about Roman London and other cities with Roman roots. I said slowly, "I don't feel at home in the country, though I know it's beautiful here."

"You loved Cornwall. I remember your father saying so. And there are ancient things there. That's one of the things I'm going to try and do before I get off the island . . . go back to Cornwall. Don't you remember the standing stones?"

I nodded. I did remember. They had been rather scary, though I had not known why.

84

"I haven't forgotten anything about that time in Cornwall," I said. "And, anyway, I wrote about it in my diary, and I still have that. That was another world. Then the war, and now, with the war ending, what's going to happen to me, stuck here with Aunt Mildred?"

"You'll get through this bit . . ."

"To what?" I asked bitterly.

"I don't know, but you'll find out. One day you'll go back to London, and you'll be an actress. Something will turn up. This is only an interlude."

"I can think of other things to call it," I said. "Your mother told me to be kind to Aunt Mildred. *Kind*. And Madame told me to learn. About other ways of life, she meant. And now you say. . . . But, when it comes to day-to-day, there does seem no future." I paused and choked a little. I knew I was talking too much about myself and my sufferings, but it *was* the first time I had spoken to anyone of my own kind. "In most ways I do wish I had died the night of the rocket."

We were in the heart of the wood. There wasn't a soul anywhere. Paul suddenly hugged me and kissed me . . . on the chin. He seemed shy, a bit embarrassed. His breath blew out in clouds and his lips were cold.

"Well, I for one am glad you didn't die. Don't forget those blue birds over the white cliffs of Dover. It seems far away now, but time does pass. There may come a day when you act in Paris, even New York. Just as I may be Paul Tremartin, the well-known archaeologist. We might appear on television."

Television. I had seen it once or twice before the war, but it was almost forgotten now.

"We won't know each other, will we?" I asked, and

85

hated the idea. Of all the people from my former life . . .

"Why not? Now let's run back through the wood. It's almost twelve-thirty. Aren't you expected home for lunch?"

I pulled myself together. That casual "Why not?" had somehow comforted me. "Yes, and you're coming, too. Whatever Aunt Mildred's faults, she won't turn away someone who had a horrid early journey from London. And she *has* met you." That dreadful morning in the Regent Palace Hotel.

So we went back, and Aunt Mildred was gracious to Paul. Katie, grumbling rather too loudly, stretched the rabbit pie to feed four instead of three. The thing that really gave me a jolt was when Aunt Mildred referred to having met Paul at the funeral. My parents' funeral, that had taken place while I lay unconscious in the gable room. Aunt Mildred was never tactful.

Robert was going down to pick something up at the station so he gave Paul a lift into Missencombe. Aunt Mildred suggested it, and telephoned Little Hartsthorn Farm. Robert had mentioned his trip the previous evening and asked if anything was wanted down in the town. Paul looked a bit startled at being given a lift by an earl, but Robert looked so ordinary he seemed reassured.

"Good-bye, Frue," he said. We had to say good-bye in public. "See you again."

But would he? When would he? After he had gone I felt bereft and went to sit in the barn with the cats.

86

8

"Get Thee to a Nunnery"

Life went on for two more days. I helped Katie indoors, Muriel outdoors, and cleaned the brasses in the tiny church. Actually I rather liked being in the church, for it was very plain, and lovely in its simplicity. The great beams of the roof were in shadow and, though it was bitterly cold, there was a feeling of peace. I didn't feel *religious*, but I was aware of the many centuries the church had stood in that little valley among the hills. Over lunch Paul had asked Aunt Mildred a number of questions, and she had answered with surprising knowledge, telling him not only of churches with Saxon and Norman work but answering some of his queries about ancient settlements.

Maybe I could get interested in such things, too. If I wanted to keep on knowing Paul (though I was buried in beechwoods and he might never come again), then I had better learn, so that I could talk intelligently. Any kind of positive aim was a comfort.

Relations were still very strained between Aunt Mildred and me. I never spoke to her if I could help it, but she was so busy always that she may not even have noticed. The strain could have been all on my side.

Then, one afternoon, Robert appeared, looking

slightly spruced up, and drove Aunt Mildred away to Hartsthorn House. I knew where they were going, but it meant nothing to me. I just supposed that Robert went to his old home sometimes and maybe Aunt Mildred liked to go, too.

When she came back at dusk she looked very pleased with herself. She sank down in the drawing room and accepted tea from Muriel.

"Well, Frue," she said, very genially, "I've just been fixing your future."

My future. As far as I knew, I hadn't one. I said nothing.

"Mrs. Hailey-Reed has just come back from her holiday. I couldn't get hold of her before. Term starts in a week, and you are to be ready by then."

"Ready?" I gaped at her.

"Uniform and everything. You're going to be a boarder at Hartsthorn House."

Hartsthorn House was still, to me, that great romantic mansion where I had been Joy in the banqueting hall and in King Henry's Garden. It was a wonderful house, but it was part of my past and not of my future. Besides, a boarding school . . . a *girls'* boarding school. Rich girls; not the kind I was used to at the Lennox, of all races and religions and kinds.

"I don't believe it!" I said.

"It's true, Frue," Muriel said, apparently thinking I was unbelieving because it was too good to be true. "We told Robert not to say anything until it was settled. There's a waiting list, but Mrs. Hailey-Reed will do anything for Robert, and she's going to squeeze you in because of the special circumstances."

"If I have to go somewhere to be educated," I said, "I'd sooner go to the high school in Missencombe, please."

There was a blank silence. Even Muriel looked hurt.

"You don't understand," Aunt Mildred said. She put down her cup, and—oh, my newly seeing eyes!—she looked very tired. "I did think of the high school, but I'm told it's very mixed. A lot of evacuees and refugees came to Missencombe, and some of them are still there. There's been trouble more than once at the high. A tough lot. . . ."

"We were very mixed at the Lennox," I said. "That's my world." And then, at last, I faced Aunt Mildred and told her the thing that gnawed at my heart. "I telephoned Madame as soon as I could get out. She told me she came here, offered me a scholarship, and said she would find me somewhere to live. And you refused."

"I refused for your own good," Aunt Mildred told me. "You had no need to be sly and go behind my back."

"But you would never have told me, and my whole life depends on being an actress."

"No, I don't expect I would have told you," Aunt Mildred agreed. She sounded quite pleasant and reasonable. "You couldn't possibly have gone back to London at this time, and you're better in health already for being here. Good country food. And as for being an actress, that can wait. You may change your mind."

"Never!" I cried dramatically. I knew I was being dramatic. There were times when I could stand outside myself.

"That's as may be. Meanwhile, your physical well-being and general education come first. You're a lucky girl, Frue. I decided I could afford Hartsthorn House for you. It's sixty pounds a term, and extras. You'll have every advantage and meet the right people. Lord Neston's girl goes there, and the daughter of the Earl and Countess of Heswall. I'm told the little Mollington girl is starting this term, so you'll be in good company."

"My great friend in London," I said, "was Kristina Manopolis. A Greek, who had been living in Italy, and she and her parents arrived penniless in London. They lived in two rooms in Chelsea. Besides, I don't want to be shut away in the beechwoods with a horde of just girls. Especially aristocratic ones. You might just as well say, 'Get thee to a nunnery!' "

"I believe they call them convents now," Aunt Mildred said, with grim humor. "Don't be ridiculous, Frue. Are you telling me you can't live without boys?"

"Well . . . maybe." I thought about it. "I'm used to having them around in school."

"I don't believe in coeducation. And you must be practical. I hope you'll change your mind, but if you mean to go on with this idea of being an actress it won't be a bad idea to have friends in high places. I seem to have heard that Lord Neston has backed several plays. They call it being an angel, I understand. And the Duke of Mollington . . ."

Oh, it was too much! I didn't make friends for such reasons. The fact that Aunt Mildred knew that much about the theatre passed me by for the moment.

"If I go to Hartsthorn House," I said, "I won't make *any* friends. I don't want that kind of friend, anyway, and if I get to be an actress it will be because I have talent and for no other reason."

Aunt Mildred actually laughed.

"It's very possible that luck, and influence, count. Go on with your tea, Frue. It's all settled, and I must write to London at once about your uniform. I'll measure you when we've finished."

"What are you going to use for coupons?" I asked, and she answered, "You got some extra ones because of what happened to you. And I bought some more."

That time she really did startle me. Aunt Mildred, so upright, a pillar of the church and a righteous citizen. It was even more surprising than her cynical knowledge of the theatre.

"You *bought* some?" All kinds of things had gone on in the Black Market for years. Once my mother bought some clothing coupons from a woman who had seven children and little money. But Aunt Mildred . . .

She was grinning . . . actually grinning. I didn't know my Aunt Mildred yet. Even Muriel laughed.

"People around here don't buy many clothes, even when they have the coupons," Aunt Mildred told me. "They were offered, and I took them. Keep your mouth shut about it. You can't go to school without the proper clothes, and it harms nobody. Finished your tea? Then where's the tape measure, Muriel? Stand up, Frue. We'll get the suit skirt a little long, as you'll grow. And the cloak long, too. The girls wear a very pretty cloak when they have to run outdoors from one building to another. The gymnasium is separate, and so is the studio. Of course there's an overcoat, too." She measured well below my knees.

"I'm to look like an orphan as well as be a nun," I said ungratefully. I was deeply upset by the turn events had taken, and to have to go to a posh school in unfashionably long clothes would be the last straw. Of course I *was* an orphan. No one in the world but Aunt Mildred and Muriel.

"The hems can be turned up temporarily," Muriel said.

"By whom?" I demanded. They both sewed badly.

"You might learn to sew yourself," Aunt Mildred said tartly.

I might, at that. Mother had learned, and she had made the green dress and my velvet skirt. The thought of my mother made me feel so sad and hopeless that I said no more, and Aunt Mildred sat down to write the letter to the London store.

The next morning I met Robert near the gate of Little Hartsthorn Farm. He was talking to a man with a great load of timber on a horse-drawn truck, but left him to come to me.

"Well, Frue, so you're going to Hartsthorn House?"

It was a gray, bitterly cold day and I was sunk in gloom, but I had decided to go for a cycle ride to look for the nearest part of Grim's Ditch. It was some kind of ancient earthwork that went for miles across the Chilterns. I could write and tell Paul about it. The one clear idea I had was that I must try and learn about things that interested him.

I had had to dismount, anyway, because the great truck blocked the lane. I leaned on the handlebars and looked up at Robert. He was quite tall. His thin face looked cold.

"Yes. Isn't it awful?"

"Your aunt thought it would be a fine thing for you."

"Well, I don't!" I exploded. "I don't want to be shut up with seventy posh girls, miles from town, or even a proper village. Never a film or a play; nothing but endless beechwoods." I never, never thought I would talk to an earl like that, or talk to an earl at all. But I was already taking Robert Speen for granted.

He laughed and glanced at the timber. "Those beechwoods are worth a mint of money and are beautiful, too."

"If they're beautiful why do you cut them down?"

"We only do it in certain places, and when the trees are a certain age. Cheer up about school, Frue. You know the house already, or have you forgotten the inside of it? I remember Joy in the banqueting hall, leaning over the gallery railings."

"You saw the film?" Everyone in the Hartsthorns had seen it, the vicar had said.

"I not only saw it," Robert told me, "but I was there during the filming. I kept in the background. The film people didn't even know I was there. But I watched those shots in the banqueting hall from the Tudor room, with the door three inches open. You were a good little actress all those years ago, and your father knew exactly what he wanted. By the way, I told Mildred that you must go on with your acting one day."

In spite of the cold wind I felt suddenly warmer.

"*Did* you? That was decent of you. But it's now that bothers me. I don't want to be safe and comfortable in the country while the war is still going on and people are suffering in London. It doesn't seem right."

Robert laughed. "Oh, as to that, you needn't worry. You'll be remarkably *uncomfortable* at school, and the food's vile, I believe."

93

"But it's sixty pounds a term, with extras on top!" I gasped, astonished. "And that ▆▆▆▆▆ little Lady Somebody and the Earl and Countess of Heswall's daughter go there. And the Mollington girl is starting this term. Her father's a *duke*, and I suppose that's higher than an earl. I wouldn't know. My father was a socialist."

He didn't seem to notice that I had sworn, and he didn't take up my challenge about my father. He laughed again, really amused.

"And a few other ladies and honorables, too," he said cheerfully. "Don't go in for inverted snobbery, Frue. They help to wash the dishes like everyone else, and sleep in unheated rooms, some of them up in the attics, where the unfortunate maids once slept. And, at the end of term, they all help to clean the whole house, and oil the paneling."

"They *don't?*"

"They do. Very little proper domestic help is kept; can't get any, of course. Two women from Hartsthorn Common do most of the cooking, and there are two or three older girls, there on reduced terms, who do some housework."

"How beastly for them." My ideas of boarding schools came from the school stories I had gone through a period of loving. Mother always said schools weren't a bit like that, but Hartsthorn House filled the bill as far as appearances went. I wondered if there were any secret passages. "I suppose the other girls give them an awful life."

"Well, they may." He seemed to think about it. "But I doubt it. They all seem nice girls. Even Lady This and That has to help in her own home nowadays. I expect they think nothing of it." He didn't say, "*I* was brought up in feudal grandeur, and took soup to the poor. I was the little Lord of the Manor at Christmas parties. I went to Eton and Oxford, and now here I am an ordinary farmer." But I remembered it. Though he wasn't quite an ordinary farmer, because his son, if he had one, would inherit a great estate, and he sat in splendor in the House of Lords.

"And be sure to watch out for cockroaches," the Earl of Hartsthorn added, rather nastily. "There are millions of them in the kitchen regions; inevitable in such an old house. Turn on the light and wait until they've scuttled."

I shuddered. I hated cockroaches. My ideas of romantic Hartsthorn House had been severely shaken, but he might be teasing me.

"Go on!" I said uncertainly.

"Fact," said Robert Speen. "Well, I hope I've cheered you up. You'll need the stamina of an ox to survive Hartsthorn. Can you get past the timber? Where are you going?"

"To look for Grim's Ditch," I told him.

"You'll have to go well into Great Hartsthorn Wood to find the best bits. Got a map?"

"Yes. I can find it. And . . . thanks for the information."

"A pleasure. Oh, by the way, talking of films, there's one on in Missencombe that Muriel said she'd like to see. Ingrid Bergman in *Gaslight*. When you get home ask her if she'd like to go tomorrow evening. Pick her up at seven-thirty."

I nodded and pushed my way past the laden truck. The horses' breath rose in clouds in the icy air. They were

95

impatiently, noisily, stamping their huge feet. I was glad to reach safety.

I rode to Hartsthorn Bottom, then began to push up into the higher hills, to Hartsthorn House, and then, passing the gate, on to Hartsthorn Common and the narrow road that bisected Great Hartsthorn Wood. I had plenty of food for thought. Robert probably *had* been teasing me. A boarding school, even in wartime, couldn't be quite like that. And how nice for Muriel to go to a film with him. It would make a break for her. Even if there was "an attraction" in London, Robert probably needed company. I certainly wouldn't forget to pass on his message.

9

I Arrive in Gallery Room

I found a section of Grim's Ditch, though, even with the map, Great Hartsthorn Wood was a bit of a nightmare. The passing of trucks laden with tree trunks had caused the paths to have deep ridges. The hollows between were filled with glutinous mud, and there were brambles and overgrown hollies that made it difficult to step aside. I was surprised at myself for venturing so far into the vast wood that was so dim and silent on that gloomy day. I must be getting used to the country.

I thought of the King's Road, Chelsea, clogged with traffic and crowded with shoppers. Something about the Chiltern country was casting a slight spell, but how desperately I longed for the life of London. It was better not to think of it.

I scrambled down into the wide, deep hollow that long ago men had dug as some kind of rampart for defense. Well, I'd found it, stood in it, and I would tell Paul. It would be an excuse for a letter. Then I rushed as fast as I dared over the uneven track back to the road and Muriel's bicycle. According to the map, the wood was riddled with paths and one went close to Hartsthorn House, a mile away.

There was almost no traffic, and the only thing that

passed me was a Farmer's bus, taking its long, wandering route over the hills to Missencombe.

I arrived back just at lunchtime and Muriel was already helping Katie to carry in the food. When we were sitting at the table I passed on Robert's message. Muriel received it with an impassive face.

"Very nice of him. I'd like to go."

"But it's the Red Cross whist drive," Aunt Mildred said, looking annoyed. "Robert must have forgotten. You must telephone him and say you can't go.

I watched interestedly. Muriel must have been to a million whist drives. I wished they would ask me to go with them to see *Gaslight*. I had missed it in London and longed to see it. But of course she would give in to her mother.

She did nothing of the kind.

"You have plenty of people to go with, Mother," she said quietly. "They'll all walk down the lane together." I knew by then that the little hall where the Red Cross met was tucked into the trees behind the forge at Hartsthorn Bottom. "I want to see that film."

"But it's not long since you went to one with him. Just before Christmas, wasn't it? Of course it's very nice of Robert, but . . ."

And Muriel, cutting her short, laughed. "That was a different film, Mother."

Good for her! I concentrated on my lunch, which was very good. The week's meat ration; the official one, that is. Rabbits came free in Little Hartsthorn. I always felt guilty about eating such appetizing food while people in the cities were, if not actually starving, extremely ill fed. But my stomach wouldn't be denied the pleasure, even when my heart was still so often aching with my sense of loss, and my mind was troubled.

Troubled . . . that rotten school. Robert must have been joking, and I would find it a haven of luxury. The girls would talk about nothing but hunting, if they came from country houses, and that sounded a cruel and beastly thing. They wouldn't know, or care, about my lost world. Rich, pampered, and seventy of them. I went hot (though the dining room was icy cold) at the very thought of being a prisoner there for three months. Aunt Mildred had said I could spend occasional weekends at Dogwood House, but what good would that be? She would only put me to digging the kitchen garden, or cleaning out the hens. Nothing, nothing to look forward to in the whole vast future. Unless Paul came again, and why should he when he was back at school, with his work and all his interests? He would forget Frue Allendale, fifteen years old, wearing a dreadful woolen helmet, a childish coat, and dirty boots. Hardly a glamour puss.

Aunt Mildred got out a big leather trunk with brass fittings. It bore an impressive array of foreign labels and she told me it had been used by her husband when he was young.

"He did a lot of traveling in those days," she said. "His parents were very well off then, and his father had business interests in many parts of the world. Cecil used to go with him."

Should *I* ever see the world, even such a changed one as would be left after the war? Paris and New York, Paul had said. Oh, to see New York, to act on Broadway, with the Empire State Building looming over Manhattan.

"I hope your school clothes come in time," Aunt Mildred said anxiously.

Meanwhile, we went down to Missencombe and she bought me all kinds of things; toiletries, house shoes, underclothes. There was one quite large store in Missencombe and we happened to pass through the dress department. There, on a model, was the prettiest party dress. It was turquoise blue, with a tight waist and a long skirt, for, in spite of shortage of materials, full-length party dresses for young people were coming in.

Aunt Mildred stopped and surveyed it, then looked at the ticket.

"Your size, Frue, and we have just about enough coupons left. Would you like to try it on?"

I was astonished. My old, short party dress had not been in the trunk that came from London. In fact, I hadn't worn it for a long time; I had grown too much. That turquoise blue dress looked fit for a princess and not for Frue Allendale, in her dreadful, shabby clothes. Try cleaning out the hens in that! But, of course I had forgotten, I was going to a swish school.

"You must have one," Aunt Mildred said impatiently, when I didn't answer. "It's on the list of required clothes. They sometimes hold impromptu dances in the banqueting hall."

Dance to your daddy, my little laddie . . . the words of the old song came into my head. Dance in the banqueting hall, where Joy had moved lightly, a small ghost.

"Thank you very much," I said. "I would like to try it on, please."

The dress was perfect. I looked at least sixteen. If only Paul could see me wearing it. I carried it home as if it were a bomb about to go off. It seemed a small miracle in a horrible wartime world. But still I dreaded going to Hartsthorn House.

Muriel dyed my dressing gown, very badly, and I inherited two rather old pairs of pajamas from her. The coupons, even Black Market ones, didn't run to everything.

My uniform came from London two days before I was to go to school. There was a dark-green flannel suit, a dark-green overcoat, a gym tunic, three white blouses, a rather queerly shaped green hat with the school badge, and the cloak. The cloak was of the same dark green, but the big loose hood was lined with brilliant blue. Blue and green were *never* put together, though I remembered Mr. Tremartin saying they should be. The cloak, enswathing me, was almost glamorous, with quite a swirl when I moved. In secret, my heart delighted in both cloak and party dress. After years of wartime shortages and economy, it was hard to resist such beauty. But going to Hartsthorn House was a high price to pay for two lovely garments.

I didn't mind the cloak being long, but the coat and the skirt of the suit, when I tried them on, filled me with despair. All my pleasure fled. I looked terrible in them. Little Orphan Annie. Aunt Mildred pinned up the hems and ordered Muriel to tack them and see what they looked like then. Muriel got them crooked and I looked worse than ever. But what did anything really matter? I would be a green nun, imprisoned in an ancient house, with cockroaches (a joke?) in the kitchen regions, and nothing but huntin', shootin', and fishin' talk. And I so much wanted, in spite of being sidetracked by cloak and dress, to be back in London, where the war was still on, but theatres were playing to packed houses.

Muriel fished out a small, flat parcel that had lain unseen at the very bottom of the box. It contained two green and white cotton overalls.

"What on earth are *they* for?"

"To protect your good clothes when you're helping in the house," Aunt Mildred told me briskly.

"So you mean Robert wasn't joking when he said the girls wash the dishes and oil the paneling and that?"

"The girls learn to be useful," Aunt Mildred said. "Excellent training. One day they'll be wives and mothers."

"You're not telling me that Lord Neston's girl will have to do her own dishwashing when the war's over?" I held the overalls against me. They came halfway down my shins. "Likely she'll marry a duke."

Aunt Mildred laughed and patted me quite playfully on the shoulder. "You have a lot to learn about life, Frue. Rich people may get back some kind of domestic staff as time goes on, but things will never be the same again."

No, they wouldn't . . . not for me, maybe not for many, many girls and boys.

Aunt Mildred ordered a taxi to take me and my trunk to Hartsthorn House. It was an awful day, sleeting and dark. The woods seemed even more brooding than usual, and the great house was almost invisible at the top of the Stretch as we drove up the narrow road.

It was three o'clock. The pig had been killed and I had eaten a pork lunch; delicious, but it didn't lie very comfortably. I was very cold, and scared, and rebellious. It was suddenly like being in a kind of nightmare. In my own world, at the Lennox, I had been confident and completely happy. I knew where I was, and where I meant to go, and each day ended with my arrival back in the mews.

But, on the way to the nunnery, I felt about ten. It really was incredible. Me, a new girl at a fashionable boarding school. For it evidently *was* fashionable, in spite of the cockroaches, the housework, and the possibly awful food.

Aunt Mildred had shown me an advertisement in a glossy magazine that said: "Hartsthorn House School . . . put your daughter on the waiting list. She will be educated by a graduate staff in beautiful surroundings. The top-ranking school in the Chilterns."

My only real comfort was that I had my secret store of money. If I hated it as much as I thought I would, I would run away to London. I was fifteen; you could leave school at fourteen. And my father had never made Aunt Mildred my official guardian. I could disappear and find work. Maybe a wild dream, but it was there in my mind as we drove past the lodge and up the beech avenue. We swung around by the church and some stable buildings and drew up at the West Front, where five great cedars brooded blackly in the dim light. Sleet blew in my face as we stepped out onto the gravel. Joy was back at Hartsthorn House and this time she was facing something very different.

Two girls wearing Land Army uniforms suddenly appeared and began to handle my trunk. "We're helping . . . it's O.K.," one said cheerily to Aunt Mildred. "They all get put in the outer hall and the girls carry their things up on trays. Mrs. Hailey-Reed won't have boxes carried upstairs. It might damage the paneling."

"Very sensible," said Aunt Mildred. "Come on, Frue." And she pushed me through a great oak door into the outer hall, where already there were several boxes, and girls wearing green suits bending over them. A woman in nurse's uniform was giving orders. She looked up briefly when we appeared.

"A new girl? Fruella Allendale? How do you do, my dear? I'm Matron. Go through into the banqueting hall, please. Miss Dook is waiting there."

We went through into the banqueting hall and the nightmare turned into a dream. The smell hit me first; a smell of old wood, and faint wood smoke and flowers. The lights were all on, and the beauty of the place was greater than I remembered. There was the portrait of Queen Elizabeth the First, and the one of the Robert Speen who had followed Hampden to Chalgrove Field. And he was like Robert the Earl, or Robert the Earl was like him. The same chin and eyes.

The flowers were early daffodils, massed in the corners, glowing gold against the ancient paneling. Daffodils in January in wartime. Above was the gallery, and there was a scuffle, and a low laugh, and a fair head thrust for a moment over the railings. My momentary pleasure died, for, as soon as Aunt Mildred had gone, I would have to face the girls and accept the fact that this was my world for three long months.

Miss Dook introduced herself as the maths mistress. She was quite young, and striking looking in a curiously old-fashioned way. She was very pale and wore no makeup at all; her bright red hair was plaited and coiled in earphones over her ears. She said Mrs. Hailey-Reed was in the Tudor Room and led us to a door in a corner.

The Tudor Room also smelled of wood smoke and daffodils, and a small fire danced on the hearth. I don't know what I expected, but Mrs. Hailey-Reed was a surprise. She was quite old, but her hair was dyed a dark blonde, and she wore a lot of make-up and stylish clothes. Towny clothes, not country. A handsome silk blouse, a well-cut skirt, and high-heeled shoes.

She came forward effusively to greet Aunt Mildred, and her voice was loud and clear and a bit overdone. "Well, Mrs. Butler, how nice to see you again. And this is Fruella? How are you, my dear? What a pale, cold child! Fifteen? Well, you'll be in the Middle School. Eleven to thirteen are Juniors, then thirteen to sixteen are Middles, and we have twenty-five Seniors all over sixteen, not including the Students, who live over in the flat with Mrs. Weston. I call her our tame author. She's helping me for a few terms until her husband gets back from the war. She's well known as the author of books for girls, and Dennis Weston was an artist until the war got him." That caught my attention . . . it sounded interesting. But she went on, "We all work hard at Hartsthorn. I hope you're a clever girl? Done some acting, I hear. You've been at the Lennox School? An excellent place. I know Madame Ramier well. I spoke to her about you, Fruella."

"*Did* you?"

"We're going to forget all that for the moment," Aunt Mildred said briskly, and I hated her. We are *not*. Fancy Mrs. Hailey-Reed knowing Madame! Come to think of it, she looked a bit like an ageing actress; there was a vague impression that she was *acting* the part of the head of a fashionable boarding school.

"Fruella is in Gallery Room. That's one of our nicest bedrooms. Matron will take her up and she can start unpacking. Today we're having a meal at five-thirty instead of the usual dinner at seven-thirty. Some of the girls have long journeys, and trains are so bad, aren't they? So often delayed, and dreadfully overcrowded, even first class, and so hard to get any food. The poor things arrive half-starved. Everyone to bed early after milk and biscuits, then ready for work tomorrow." Her voice rang out.

"I'm sure everything will be splendid, Mrs. Hailey-Reed," Aunt Mildred said. She seemed subdued by what seemed a stronger personality. At any rate, a more flamboyant one.

Even hating Aunt Mildred, I had a sudden impulse to fling myself at her and beg her to take me home. The girls in Gallery Room would want to know all about me and I would have to speak of the night of the rocket. But I couldn't. I wouldn't tell them. It was still too recent, and too painful.

Mrs. Hailey-Reed accompanied us out into the banqueting hall, and Miss Dook advanced with a tall, middle-aged man with an anxious face. At his side was a very small girl whose uniform was much too big, and her hat half-buried her pale, thin little face. Mrs. Hailey-Reed forgot Aunt Mildred and went forward gushingly. "Well, so you've brought Annabella? Did you have a terrible journey from Mollington? Do come to the fire in the Tudor Room."

Forgotten, Aunt Mildred and I looked at each other.

"The Duke of Mollington," Aunt Mildred murmured. "I met him once at a flower show. And that's the little Lady Annabella. I heard . . . but it was gossip."

The little Lady Annabella had looked even more of an Orphan Annie than I did. She couldn't be a day over nine, poor little scrap. Thoughts of the other girl carried me through Miss Dook's quick switch of us from the banqueting hall to Matron in the outer hall. I scarcely had a chance to say good-bye to Aunt Mildred, who hurried away to the expensive, waiting taxi.

My trunk had been put in the kitchen passage, with others that were arriving. Matron had decided that there were enough in the outer hall. I thought, with a shudder, of the millions of cockroaches. It seemed very possible that they were lurking somewhere. The passage was wide and very long and dim. The floor was of ancient flagstones, and there were blackened beams overhead. Here and there a bare electric light bulb pierced the gloom. There was a strong smell of damp. Clearly great houses had other aspects than their romantic hearts.

Matron snatched my keys, opened the trunk, and took up the overloaded top tray. "I'll bring this for you, Fruella, and then you must carry what you can each trip. Follow me."

I followed. There were girls everywhere, chattering, laughing, and talking in high, clear voices. Lovely voices. I had to admit. The kind of voice I could assume in a play, but usually I knew I was a bit Cockney. And I'd stay Cockney! I wasn't going to pretend anything, except that I didn't want to tell them about London.

Hartsthorn House was cold. The kitchen passage was icy, and the back stairs had a stiff draught blowing from somewhere. After a few moments we emerged onto the gallery that ran around the banqueting hall. Below, that lovely great room looked like an oasis of beauty.

Gallery Room was very large; probably it had been the master bedroom when the house was a home. I must ask Robert. The other girls had already arrived and were settling in. For a moment I thought there were a dozen; then I counted seven. I shrank in the bright light. It was awful. *Just* like a school story. The new girl. The strange faces all swung around to stare at me. Seven heads of different colored hair . . . some long, some short.

There were no curtains, no cubicles, such as I had hoped for; not one speck of privacy. Eight small, plain beds; eight little dressing-tables, with drawers; one whole side of the room taken up by two huge wardrobes and four fitted wash basins.

"This is Fruella Allendale," Matron said briskly, and the girls all said "How do you do?" politely. We were never very polite at the Lennox School, though friendly. Some of the foreign pupils couldn't speak English too well.

"That's your bed in the corner over there," Matron went on. "Next to Richenda. You tell her about everything, Richenda, please. I'm busy. But first she must come down again and get that trunk emptied." She ladled my possessions rapidly and neatly onto the bed and handed me the top tray of my trunk.

Yes, I must get it emptied before any cockroaches decided to nest in my clothes. I rushed down the back stairs, clutching the unwieldy tray. When I returned the girls all surrounded me.

"We go in for unusual names here," the girl called

Richenda said. She was tall and very thin, with straight, bright brown hair. Her suit was too short and very shabby. Mine was spanking new and still too long. "Fruella . . . that's a new one. Do they call you all that?"

"I'm Frue."

They all began to ask questions. Where I lived, what school I had been to before. They seemed friendly, but I felt beset. I couldn't believe I was at Hartsthorn House, with the darkening woods stretching for miles outside.

10

Boarding School in Wartime

I said desperately to the ring of curious faces, "I live at Dogwood House, Little Hartsthorn, with my great aunt, Mrs. Cecil Butler. Before that I was at school in London."

There was a silence. Maybe they had sensed that I didn't want to talk about it. Then a girl with dark, sleek hair and a very attractive face seized the tray from me and began to dispose of my possessions very rapidly and neatly. Underclothes, stockings, handkerchiefs went into drawers. While she worked she said, "Dogwood House? They tell me the dogwood trees are lovely in the spring. I only came here in September. That's near, isn't it? Only a mile or two? Bobby Earl lives at Little Hartsthorn. Do you know him?"

The others were all busy putting away their clothes, and the awful moment had passed. I felt a trifle more relaxed.

"Yes, I know him. He's a friend of my Aunt Mildred's."

"Lucky you! He's rather a dish, don't you think?"

"He's all right." I was annoyed that I seemed to be cashing in on my acquaintance with Robert.

"He's one of the few men we see around here," the

dark girl said, and giggled. There was a chorus of, "Except the vicar and the garden boys, Jemima."

"Don't forget the butcher's boy!"

"He squints. I draw the line at Ben."

"Get thee to a nunnery!" That was about right. I escaped to fetch more of my possessions and, when I returned, they were all talking hard and seemed to have forgotten me. My worst fears were realized, it seemed. The talk was all about what they had done in the holidays. They had evidently had a very social time. Parties, theatres, riding. The girl called Richenda had a new mare. They talked about clothes, grumbling about lack of coupons, and about the boys and young men they had met.

Forgotten, I began to put away the rest of my clothes. My heart was sore and lonely. Paul . . . gray-faced on a cold morning. I wanted his company desperately. I even longed to be back at Dogwood House in my gable room, where at least there was privacy. I wanted young company, but of my own kind, who understood the bitter, frightening, exciting life in London. I hated to sleep with seven girls with high, clear voices, who never once spoke directly of the war.

I reminded myself that I had learned, in Little Hartsthorn, that people had suffered loss. Maybe these girls had, too. But surely never such violent, instant loss as I had experienced on the night of the rocket.

It was only four o'clock when my last tray was empty. I was just going to carry it downstairs when Richenda said, "I wonder how you'll enjoy the madhouse, Frue. Oh, don't look like that . . . it's fun, really. We never complain to our parents. Lots of things balance the food

112

and the cold and all the dotty people."

"Dotty?" I paused, arrested.

"Well, a bit off, you know. Some of them. Mrs. Hailey-Reed, for a start. She likes us to be emotional. If you want to be approved of, have roaring hysterics in the banqueting hall."

"Oh, Richenda!" A laughing chorus.

"Well, she thrives on it. She was in the chorus, you know, and all set for stardom, but she met a rich businessman. Not young, and not handsome, by all accounts, but stinking rich. He owned some night clubs, and after he died she ran them for a while. Then someone suggested she start a school. By then she was well in with the peerage and . . . well, here we all are."

It might be true, but I was not sure if I was being teased.

"Who else is dotty?"

"Well, let's say a bit unusual. It makes life interesting. There's a real-life author over at the flat. Mary Anne Angus."

"Mary Anne Angus!" She was one of the up-and-coming writers for young people. Well, maybe she had arrived. I knew her books quite well. They were not ordinary. They did not fall into any of the conventional categories. Mrs. Weston, Mrs. Hailey-Reed had said. "Is she the one whose husband is the artist, Dennis Weston?"

"Yes. She's had a bad war. Her husband was reported missing, believed killed, but he turned up later. They're still madly in love, we guess. But she doesn't say much, except that she tells the Juniors stories on the nights she takes over from Matron over here. Miss Dook is an odd bod; very righteous. Her father is Icelandic or something and some kind of low church minister. She and her friend Jane Short, the English mistress, have the most violent rows. Mademoiselle Granier has a lover down in Burley's Bottom. A farm worker . . . imagine it!"

"*Richenda!*"

"Well, she has to have some compensation for being cooped up here for three months at a time. Soon as the war's over she'll go back to Paris. I hope you don't mind mice," Richenda ended pleasantly, looking at me. "For they add to the fun. Miss Short goes crazy at the sight of one, and there are hundreds."

"No," I said, hoping I was playing her game. "I think they're really quite sweet." And I escaped, closing the door behind me. Pinned to the outside of the door was a "newly arrived" list of names. Gabrielle Raine, Joanna Puckworthy, Richenda Neston—Lord Neston's girl?—Dawn Willis-Carr, Marilyn Blakeley, Jemima Herriot-Lane, Miranda Churley, Fruella Allendale. The dark girl who had helped me was Jemima. I thought she might be a lot nicer than Richenda, who was amusing but too much for me.

It was *all* too much for me. Oh, God, three months of it! Slowly I went down the back stairs. More and more trunks were arriving and green-clad girls were everywhere. I put back my tray and closed my trunk. I wouldn't see it again until the end of term.

No one took any notice of me. In the banqueting hall, Miss Dook was greeting new parents. I slipped past, looking for somewhere to hide. At the far end of the great hall, between the portraits of Elizabeth and Robert Speen, was an oak door, half-hidden in the paneling.

Guiltily I opened it, and slipped into a dark room. Grouping around, I found a light switch, and the soft glow revealed a little paneled room, scantily furnished. There was an upright piano, a music stand, and piles of music on a low oak table. There was also an ancient oak settle and, on the settle, in a small heap, was a figure wearing the school suit. Startled by the light, she tossed back untidy brown hair and raised a small, tear-stained face.

"You're . . . Annabella!" I said. The Lady Annabella, daughter of a duke, but the most miserable little kid I had ever seen. "Why are you here alone? Isn't someone looking after you?"

"Y-yes, some girl. I . . . I got away. I w-wanted to be alone."

"That makes two of us," I said grimly, and sat down on the settle beside her. "I'm Frue Allendale. I'm new, too, and I didn't want to come. It's all pretty strange, isn't it? But *you* seem too young to be here."

She sniffed, and coughed, and groped for a handkerchief.

"I'm just t-ten. Mrs. Hailey-Reed said she'd take me, as a special favor. I'm s-supposed to be in the little drawing room with the Juniors."

Oh, so we used the drawing rooms as sitting rooms; those great Adams rooms along the East Front that I remembered. Very elegant, and very suitable for a duke's daughter. *I* would have given anything to be at the shabby and scruffy Lennox School, in its new quarters in a dreary part of Kensington.

Tact made me refrain from further questions. She was so clearly in worse trouble than I was, or less able to cope

115

with it. But she said shakily, "I had to come to school. My governess has married an airman, and my m-mother has *gone away!*" The last in a high wail.

The Duchess of Mollington.... During the last weeks I had read the papers mainly for war news, and for reviews of plays. But I suddenly remembered that I had seen something in a gossip column: "The Duchess of Mollington was seen at Le Beau Cheval with an interesting new escort. Rumor has it that her marriage to the Duke is about to come to an end." Poor little Annabella! It wasn't as bad as seeing her mother, in a green dress, sitting dead in firelight. But it was bad enough.

"Hard luck!" I said awkwardly. She didn't seem to find it inadequate. She nestled against me, sniffing rhythmically.

"I wish I were *dead!*"

"I said that only a few weeks ago," I told her. "But it's no good, is it? We're alive, and you may like it here. It's a beautiful house."

"Nicer than Mollington," she said, with a gulp. "Mollington's so huge and cold . . . a castle, really. Of course the Army has most of it. We live in the West Wing. When the war is over Daddy's going to build a little house for us in the park. He says it will never be easy to live in castles again. Do you live in a castle?"

"I do not," I said. "I live with my aunt near here. I have no money; not much, anyway. Cheer up, Annabella. It may not be so bad." It was more likely to be her world than mine.

"Daddy calls me Annie." Good heavens! Not pretty, but it suited her all right. I didn't speak, and she went on, "I like you. Will you be my friend?"

I had gone to Hartsthorn with the fixed intention of making no friends. After what Aunt Mildred had said I felt I hardly could, for she would think of every family in terms of what I might one day get out of them. I meant to stay a solitary observer, alone in my unhappiness, and now here was this child, this unfortunate aristocratic child, nestling against me as if she were my little sister. Most disconcerting of all, I felt a sudden surge of warmth, a real human desire to comfort her. But it couldn't be done. She had to find friends of her own age, or as near it as possible.

"Look, Annabella, I can't be your friend," I said. "I expect we'll hardly meet, once the term really starts."

She gulped and clung to me. "But I *want* you to be, Frue. I'm in Junior Bedroom Two, and there are seven others, but my bed is near the door. You could kiss me good night, the way Nannie does at home."

Oh, so there was a nannie, too . . . definitely out of my world. But kisses were common to everyone.

The door opened and Miss Dook stood there. "Fruella, I saw you sneak in here. And Annabella. You two girls should be in the drawing rooms if you've finished unpacking. Come along with me."

Ignoring Annabella's tear-stained face, she led us out through the banqueting hall and called a passing Junior to take Annabella to where she ought to be. I was taken to the door of one of the middle drawing rooms and told to stay there until the gong sounded.

The ornate moldings, the gorgeous wallpaper, the Adams fireplace were the same, but the elegant, valuable furniture had gone. There were folding desks and chairs piled up in a corner, a long line of bookcases, and, around a very small wood fire, a huddle of girls, some sitting in comfortable chairs, others sprawled on the floor. There seemed to be heating pipes around the room, but the place was extremely cold. The long curtains had been drawn against the fast-coming winter night.

No one seemed to notice my advent. I went over to the bookcases, chose a book called *Chiltern Country*, and sat on the floor, pretending to read. But really I was fighting such deep despair that I wished I could cry like Annabella.

Bits of conversation from the big group around the fire came to me occasionally. It was the same old thing, holiday chat. But after a time some light-hearted grumbles. Much more interesting to me.

"Just fancy, girls! Back in this hole for three long months. I hope it's not my turn to scrape nearly a hundred disgusting plates tonight."

"I hope it's not *my* turn to help wash them. It absolutely turns me up to wash those mountains of dishes in nearly cold water. It's completely unhygienic."

"I bet supper will be awful. Do you remember that last meal we had before Christmas? It was horse meat for sure."

"Some people say horse meat can be very tasty. If you were starving you'd enjoy it."

"Ugh, I shouldn't. I think Mrs. H-R uses our ration books to buy wonderful meals for herself."

"And eats them in secret in the Tudor Room!" There was a shout of laughter.

"But who cooks them?"

"*She* does, at dead of night, braving the cockroaches."

No, Robert had not been teasing me. Much of it was

evidently the simple truth. At that moment the girl called Jemima came in, saw me alone, and came over to me.

"Aren't you frozen, Frue? Do come to the fire and meet everyone."

"In a minute," I muttered. The other members of Gallery Room seemed now to have appeared, and they were all pushing for places near the fire. I knew that they would be friendly if I went over and joined them, but I felt so unhappy, prickly and out of place, that I stayed where I was until, at last, a gong sounded and they all sprang to their feet.

I followed them into the banqueting hall. Girls were pouring from all directions and forming two lines down the whole length of the room, facing each other. And, between the lines, walking as if under triumphal arches, came the members of the staff, each woman bearing a jam jar and a dish with butter or margarine on it. It really looked funny, but everyone seemed to take it for granted. What a scene for that glorious hall to witness! Yet, comical as it was, it was a scene of war, illustrating wartime shortages, and Hartsthorn House had certainly known other aspects of war. Aunt Mildred had said something about the Robert Speen of Civil War times being captured by the Royalists in a little room off the banqueting hall that was called the Captivity Parlor to this day. Maybe it was the little music room where Annabella and I had hidden. Robert Speen had escaped to join John Hampden and the Parliamentary forces and to die on Chalgrove Field. For a moment I saw, not the absurd line of women heading for the dining room, but the Royalist soldiers, and Robert Speen, whose face still looked down at us, held between two of them, a prisoner in his own house. Later his body had been brought there from the battlefield.

Everything passed. Queen Elizabeth had gone centuries ago, and Robert Speen was only a faintly heroic figure in history. Speen upon Speen, you might say, down the ages, suffering, loving, fighting, perhaps merely hearing war news in that great and wonderful hall. *My* Robert Speen had seen the beginning of the present war in his own house, but he had gone to Little Hartsthorn by the time France fell and the war became the scary, desperate business it had been for so many years. And now precious pots of jam and two ounces of margarine were borne through the banqueting hall like heads on platters.

I, too, would pass. I was there, lonely and observing and unhappy, but one day I would be gone into that unknown, maybe nonexistent, place to which my father and mother had been so abruptly banished.

It was fascinating to watch the present scene. That must be Mademoiselle Granier. She had a French face and figure and was beautiful, in a way, in spite of what seemed to be *three* dreadful sweaters. It couldn't be true about the farm laborer down in Burley's Bottom.

"Come *on*, Frue!" Richenda prodded me. We turned and walked into a huge, cold dining room with paneled walls on which still hung some Speen family portraits. Several long tables ran the length of the room, with the staff table at the top. The whole school was there, and various other people, including the Land Girls and two cold-looking boys.

Mrs. Hailey-Reed came in last and took her place in

the middle of the staff table. Two or three girls from each table fetched the food from a serving hatch. It was some kind of cheese pie, and looked rather nasty, but it was better than suspecting horse. Robert the Earl had not exaggerated. There was plenty of bread, and everyone filled up with that. Afterward there were stewed blackberries, all pitty and gritty and very sour.

My seeing eyes kept on working overtime, in spite of my misery. There were ten members of the staff, including Matron, and most of them looked cold and rather cross. Next to Mrs. Hailey-Reed sat a very good-looking, dark-haired woman wearing a smart suit with the square shoulders that were in vogue. Richenda told me that she was the secretary, Mrs. Gaye. "She was an officer in the WAAF, but she had an illness and was demobbed. If she still has a husband she never speaks of him. We like her; she's fun."

There were about twenty people at my table and, down at the other end, was a face that seemed faintly familiar. She was a pale girl, with high cheekbones and quite long dark brown hair. The more I looked the more I felt I knew her, yet I could not possibly know any girl at Hartsthorn House.

"Who's that?" I asked Richenda. "That dark girl at the bottom righthand corner of the table."

"Nicola Kelsey. She's a Middle and sleeps in the big East bedroom. Quite nice, but rather quiet. Comes from London, I think. I seem to have heard they've been bombed twice."

Nicola was now looking up the table straight at me. Embarrassed, I dropped my gaze. I couldn't possibly know her.

By seven-thirty the Juniors had gone to bed, and it was bedtime for Middles and Seniors at eight o'clock. I dreaded Gallery Room and no privacy at all. I was not used to washing and undressing in front of a crowd of strangers. By then I was very cold, had slight indigestion, and was so sunk in depression I hardly knew what to do.

I went cautiously upstairs before the bell. The banqueting hall was deserted and dimly lighted. I leaned on the gallery railing and looked down. Oh, most beautiful place! It seemed incredible that it could lie, serene and sweet smelling, in the middle of so much that was unbearable. There my father had worked, there I had been Joy, there Robert the Earl had watched from behind the Tudor Room door. So long ago, before Cornwall, before the war.

I found Junior Room Two around the corner, in a wide corridor. The name was on the door, which was a little open. Hardly thinking, I crept in. A nightlight was burning and everyone seemed to be asleep. I could just see Annabella in the bed nearest the door. *She* was not asleep; she turned quickly toward me, and her face was wet with tears.

"Good night," I whispered. "Just this first night. I can't do it again. Are you O.K?"

"Um!" She tried to hold me. Dear Heaven, I wasn't Nannie. What had possessed me? I went to Gallery Room, and was washed and in bed before the other seven came upstairs.

\ 11 /

I Do a Foolish Thing

Nearly three weeks passed in a kind of limbo. It was all my fault. Everyone was perfectly nice to me, and I would have been accepted without question if I had been more outgoing. The girls in Gallery Room were probably puzzled by my withdrawal, but they didn't let it bother them. After a week or two they left me to myself, more or less. I always got into bed as quickly as I could and sat there until Lights Out, writing in my diary; then I huddled under the bedclothes, shivering, for the weather was icy outdoors, and Gallery Room was scarcely less cold. The others seemed much tougher than I was and would wander around with nothing on . . . not a stitch. They were all quite unselfconscious, whereas I hated to be seen naked. I was ashamed of my feelings, for they did seem silly, and nothing in my upbringing had made me believe that nakedness was wrong.

All the same, I was always surprised at the natural way they would stop and chat during their ablutions at the wash basins, even when Matron came in, or Mary Anne Angus, on the nights she saw the whole school to bed.

She seemed to me the one truly interesting person in the place, maybe because she was an author. I understood acting, but I did not understand writing books. It seemed a strange and secret thing. She was about thirty, slim and brown haired, with horn-rimmed glasses. Rumor said she had had a lot of eye trouble. She had a very attractive face, though she was not pretty, and she looked warm and alive, though sometimes sad when she thought no one was looking at her. No one else among the staff looked particularly warm and alive. I got the impression that they did not greatly care for being in a nunnery, either, eating awful food and doing constant duties out of actual lesson hours.

"Give them a chance and they're off to the Beech-tree Inn at Hartsthorn Common," Jemima said. "Out of bounds, even for Students. Mrs. Dean there does ham and eggs . . . imagine it! But Jane Short is scared of the dark lanes. She and Dook had a fierce quarrel about it yesterday."

Miss Short, who taught English, didn't appeal to me, but I sympathized with anyone who found the absolutely black countryside frightening. I had never grown used to it while I was at Little Hartsthorn. Once darkness had fallen I felt besieged. Yet it was silly, for London had been pretty dark all through the war and I took that for granted. It was the feeling that, in those ancient hills, unknown "things" came closer. A tribute, I suppose, to the haunted quality of that beautiful, remote countryside, where history went back far, far beyond record.

It was a hard life at Hartsthorn House. We rose at seven, washed in cold water and dressed at speed. According to the timetable, some had to practice the piano in the various music rooms while others went over to the gymnasium for drill. Breakfast at eight, after brief prayers in the banqueting hall; then, if the weather was not actually impossible, a run up the drive before lessons. As it was only just growing light and was always bitterly cold, I hated that particular exercise. I yearned for the enclosed comfort of our house in the mews and my short journey to the Lennox after a peaceful breakfast.

The only thing that got one out of the run up the drive was an after-breakfast domestic duty—scraping plates, washing the dishes, or sweeping the dining room. Scraping the plates into the pig buckets was the worst task of all, especially if the porridge had been burned or lumpy and most people had left some. One morning about a week after my arrival I found it so disgusting that I had to flee to the nearest lavatory to be sick. I gasped and heaved, shaking and deadly cold but with sweat on my forehead.

The door didn't lock, and suddenly it opened and a brisk voice demanded, "What on earth's made you sick, Fruella?"

"The p-plates . . . I can't bear scraping them." I heaved again.

It was Miss Body, June Body, very aptly named. She was the gym and games mistress, and had come fresh from Bedford College in the autumn. She was only twenty-one; the hearty, healthy type, who believed in "no nonsense." Pink face, crisp hair, a trifle too plump for her calling. I had never met anyone like her before, and hated her more than anyone else at Hartsthorn.

"What? Oh, don't be silly, child! A few plates . . ."

"There were nearly a hundred." Rage made me forget my sickness. No one spoke to the students at the Lennox in that tone, and she was barely six years older than I.

"Well, what you need is some good fresh air. Put on your coat and run up the drive. You just have time."

"I w-want to go to bed. I'm ill." I *felt* ill.

"Rubbish! Off you go, and breathe deeply."

I obeyed and the air did smell good outdoors. I told Jemima and she said, "She's a beast! The whole thing is sublimation. She's bursting with sex, so she works it off in physical exercise and expects us to do the same."

"Oh, Jemima, she can't be!" June Body seemed to me the least sexy person I had ever met.

"True. I read a gorgeous book on psychology during the holidays."

We worked hard at Hartsthorn House; the teaching, I soon found, was of a very high standard. I had to use every scrap of brain I possessed to keep up. Only pride made me do it. We had visiting teachers from Missencombe for art, music, and singing, and Aunt Mildred had arranged for me to take all the extra subjects.

I had never played games, and hated the very idea, but I had to play hockey twice a week on a field near the house. It was muddy and awful and I was no good. Miss Body raced about, blowing a whistle and yelling encouragement. Actually, no one seemed to like it very much, and she said we were an unsporting lot.

There was hardly any chance to be alone; we were kept at it every hour of the day. So I was always a bit tired, as well as cold, rather hungry, and oh, so desolate. But rebellion burned in my heart. We rarely saw a newspaper, and only one girl had a portable radio. Life was narrowed down to the people in that great house, and inevitably there was a certain amount of tension, and things that seemed to me small were blown up sky high.

Truly Mrs. Hailey-Reed didn't mind emotionalism. She often created it. Her voice would ring through the banqueting hall on innumerable occasions. If some Juniors made an unseemly noise it was: "Oh, my dearest children, have you no feeling for atmosphere? This beautiful place, and you run and scream like hooligans. But I'm sure you were just thoughtless. Tell me you'll remember in future." And the poor kids, almost crying, would grovel and be soothed and petted.

She had a nasty way of demanding something suddenly, like the time she pounced on Miranda from Gallery Room and said, "We mustn't forget the *poetry* of life, must we? Run up to the gallery and lean over the railing and sing something to us."

Miranda, who had the best voice in the school, took it quite calmly and asked, "What shall I sing, Mrs. Hailey-Reed?"

"Something from the heart, dear child. From the heart."

Miranda's heart made her sing *Where Daisies Pied* and somehow it was very moving. Mrs. Hailey-Reed seemed to me to be wasted at Hartsthorn; she was more dramatically inclined than Madame at the Lennox. But she always made me uneasy, in case she might fasten on me. But, either from tact or because she had forgotten me, she left me alone.

Mostly, though, it was cold, discomfort, bad food, and hard work. And, worst of all, the feeling that I was a prisoner, cut off from the real world, where the war was still going on. Only the Seniors and Students were allowed out alone; the rest of us were taken for occasional walks before darkness fell on those winter afternoons.

We walked through the endless beechwoods, and sometimes to farms to collect eggs, but always in groups. I trailed behind, with cold feet and fingers, while the rest chattered. I had almost forgotten that I was supposed to be learning from new experiences, and there was no chance to find ancient sites, so that I could write and tell Paul. Daily I looked for a letter from him, but none came.

Annabella did not seem much happier than I was. She was at least a year younger than the youngest Junior, and very childish, even for ten. She was my only real contact in the school, because she still persisted in thinking of me as her friend. If she had the chance she would sneak up to me and talk about Mollington, and beg me to kiss her good night again. I did it occasionally, secretly and with some shame.

Gradually I fastened on the idea of running away to London, to Madame, to beg her to keep me and negotiate with Aunt Mildred. If Madame saw me, heard my story . . . and I had plenty of money for the journey. Escape might not be easy. I had heard that the woman at the lodge had sharp eyes and had once reported an unfortunate girl who had tried to run away. So I would have to go through Great Hartsthorn Wood and catch a Farmer's bus. I remembered the exact time one had passed me on that morning when I went to look for Grim's Ditch.

Getting away from the house would be the hardest part, but I could plead a headache and leave my class, then hope everyone would be too busy to notice.

I know it was a crazy idea; I knew it then. It was also unkind to Aunt Mildred, who had paid in advance for my first term. But the feeling of being imprisoned in that great house, in dark winter weather, was so unbearable that I knew I had to try to get away. Just to see if it could be done.

The night before I planned to go we were suddenly told there would be a dance in the banqueting hall. Mrs. Hailey-Reed had visitors, and it would be nice for them to see us having a good time. So dinner was early, and preparation was excused. We were ordered to put on our party dresses and assemble in the banqueting hall.

My blue dress was certainly one of the prettiest, but it was cold covering and I shivered. If I danced at all I wanted it to be ballet on a West End stage, or just at the Lennox in the studio with the others. In my loneliness at Hartsthorn, I thought of the Lennox constantly.

All the girls in Gallery Room had long dresses, mainly inherited from mothers or older sisters. They forgot that I was unfriendly and surrounded me.

"Oh, Frue, it's gorgeous! How did your aunt manage it?"

I began to say that I had had some extra coupons, then stopped abruptly, for that way lay danger. They would ask why, and I still couldn't bring myself to speak of the night of the rocket.

I was saved by a Senior who put her head around the door and told us to go down to the banqueting hall. Already music was rising to the gallery above; Mademoiselle was at the piano, playing a waltz. As the crowd went toward the stairs I lingered behind, and I was still on the gallery when the many colored throng took partners and began to dance.

Cold, cockroaches, mice, and nasty food faded into

insignificance, and for a few enchanted moments I was in love with Hartsthorn House, as I had felt as a young child. In that Tudor hall Queen Elizabeth had danced, and now her painted face watched the girls of 1945, with their flying hair and makeshift dresses. The evocative tune brought tears to my eyes. I couldn't *bear* to hear music at that time.

Tomorrow night I would be in some other place. Maybe with Madame at the Lennox, maybe with the Tremartins, for I had their address. They were over-crowded, Paul had said, but they would let me sleep on a couch if necessary. I might never see Hartsthorn again. Aunt Mildred would probably be so disgusted with me that she would wash her hands of me. And a girl who ran away to London would probably be such a disgrace to a fashionable school that Mrs. Hailey-Reed might conveniently expel me.

A hand on my shoulder made me jump and blink. A very nice voice said in my ear, "Do come down and dance with me, Frue."

I turned and it was Nicola Kelsey, the girl I had asked about during my first meal at Hartsthorn. Since then, though we were in many of the same classes, and had been on the same walks, we had only exchanged a few words. Yet I had often been conscious that she was looking at me, and I still had the vague, haunting feeling that I knew her.

She was about my age, but taller and very slim, and she had such an interesting face.

"I . . . I wasn't going to dance," I said. But somehow I did want to, with her.

"Oh, yes, you must. Why, you look like a dancer; I've

130

often noticed the way you move. I wish you were in our room and not with that crowd in Gallery." And she took my hand and hurried me down the drafty back stairs and through a door into the banqueting hall. As we began to dance I saw Mrs. Hailey-Reed in a corner, with several people. Among them was Robert the Earl, very spruce in one of his town suits.

Nicola stuck to me and we danced three times. My tense body began to relax and I was warm. During our third dance Robert was dancing with Mrs. Hailey-Reed, but when the music stopped he led her back to her corner, then came straight across the hall to me.

"Dance with me, Frue," he said, and whirled me into the crowd. He danced well, which was somehow surprising; after all, I had first seen him with a cartload of turnips. Yet there must have been many grand dances in his own time in that house, as well as all those visits he had paid to other great houses and castles. When we passed close under the portrait of that other Robert Speen the likeness was uncanny. It must be strange to know that your features had come down the centuries. By then I had learned that the Speens often married cousins, and Richenda had once said in a very knowing voice, "Of course, they're inbred. Bobby Earl ought to marry a strapping farmer's daughter. That would restore the balance."

But there was the "attraction" in London. She was probably a society girl, if there still were any in wartime. A society *woman*, more likely, though he was nice enough to attract a young girl, I thought, feeling very worldly. And who would refuse to be the Countess of Hartsthorn? Only how sad that their children would not

131

be brought up in that house. Senior girls in the cold attics, not housemaids; and the old nursery wing was Matron's domain, with the big night nursery used as a sick room.

We danced twice around the hall before Robert spoke. Then he asked, "Well, are you uncomfortable enough here?"

"I'm *too* uncomfortable," I said into his chest. He loomed well above me. "I must have been *mad* to say what I did. You were quite right; heaps of it is awful. But," honesty made me add, "in spite of everything, I love your house. You must mind terribly losing it."

To my surprise, he laughed. "Not at all. I was glad to see the back of it. A millstone around my neck."

"But all your ancestors . . . dancing here. Living here."

"One can't live on ancestors, Frue. I prefer living at Little Hartsthorn Farm."

"With Nannie," I said, then felt I had been rude. But he laughed and agreed.

"Nannie's very efficient. Frue, aren't you happy here?"

"No," I said, guiltily remembering my plans for the next day. "They're not my kind . . . never can be."

"Have you tried?"

"Not really. I know they'd be friendly, but . . ."

The dance came to an end and Robert led me politely to a chair by the great empty fireplace. Mrs. Hailey-Reed promptly bore him away, and after that he danced with the visitors. I was dimly aware that I had scored the hit of the evening. At least they knew I had told the truth. I knew Robert the Earl all right.

I refused offers of partners and stood watching. Dook

132

and Short were dancing together; Dook danced very badly, as if she thought it sinful. So many women under one roof. But tomorrow I would be gone.

I awoke with a headache, and it was an awful day; snowing slightly, and misty with it. But I was confident that I could find my way through Great Hartsthorn Wood to the road and went on grimly with my plan. It was unexpectedly easy. My genuine headache had made me look paler than usual, and I was given leave to stop work and go to Matron for aspirin. Instead I went to the cloakroom and put on my hat and coat and boots. The only thing I took with me was my diary, which I had hidden in my locker, and, in my diary, my paper money. I had plenty of change in my pocket for the bus.

I left by a door on the north side of the house and was soon in the shrubbery, skirting the gymnasium, the studio, and a new block of rooms where some members of the staff slept. I didn't see a soul as I slipped behind the cedars and gained the field path that headed straight toward the wood.

The snow was only falling lightly, but it was still very misty. However, I had an hour before the bus would pass, and it was only about a mile. By then I had been in the wood many times and I thought I knew the nearer paths and the one that I should take over to the road, but the snow was confusing and the mud underfoot was treacherous. After forty minutes of struggle I was afraid that I was lost.

Fifteen minutes later I was sure of it, and knew that the bus would pass without picking me up. The snow was falling faster and the flakes were quite thick. My diary was safely buttoned into my coat, but the coat itself was getting wet. My eyes were stinging with the cold flakes that were now managing to penetrate more and more steadily through the high, bare branches of the beeches.

I had thought I was used to the woods, but by then I was scared. The silence . . . the whiteness . . . the intense cold . . . I could go on wandering, struggling, for hours, and get nowhere. The only habitation actually close to the wood was Hartsthorn House, but I had no idea by then in which direction it lay. I couldn't go back if I wanted to; I was hopelessly lost.

12

The Subject of Love

It was a great relief when I stumbled upon a deserted bodger encampment. They were only crude huts, open at each end, but I would be sheltered from the snowstorm. I crept into the hut that held the motionless pole lathe and sank down, panting and dead tired, on a pile of beautifully curved chair legs. They were packed up so well that only one rolled away.

I knew then, with a burst of complete honesty, that I had behaved with total lack of sense, and unkindly, too. For Mrs. Hailey-Reed would be frantic with worry when my absence was discovered, and she would telephone Aunt Mildred. It was the craziest thing I had ever done in my life, but then I had never had to do crazy things in my *other* life, where I had been happy.

After all, they had been friendly in Gallery Room last night and this morning. Impressed because Robert had danced with me . . . well, O.K., it *was* a bit impressive to dance with an earl in his own beautiful house. And I liked Robert, so why should I be ashamed of his friendship? Inverted snobbery!

And now I was probably going to freeze to death in Great Hartsthorn Wood. Anyone who said Britain was overpopulated was out of his mind. He had never seen the Chilterns, and not much more than thirty miles from London, either.

I got up and stamped around as well as I could in the confined space. Would they have missed me at school? *When* would they miss me? I was supposed to have gone to Matron. Maybe everyone would assume that she had put me to bed in the old night nursery, and if no one asked her . . .

It was twelve-thirty, then one o'clock. The snow had settled thickly, even in the heart of the wood, and a high moaning told me that the wind was rising. Even when they found I was missing, they would think the woman at the lodge had not seen me pass and that I was already far away. They would not search the wood.

Another hour passed. In that white, cold nightmare I felt I was losing all identity. The snow had almost stopped falling, which was a small relief, but the wind was blowing it into deep drifts around my shelter. And then, suddenly, I heard voices calling: "Frue! Fruella! Frue, are you here?"

I banged my head quite violently as I left the shelter, and then found myself floundering in deep snow on top of thick mud. I shouted, "I'm here! Help!"

At first no one seemed to hear me, and I shouted again. I could hardly believe it when a girl in the Hartsthorn cloak came around a holly bush. It was Nicola.

"Frue!" She ran toward me, floundered into a drift, and we fell into each other's arms. "Oh, you fool!" she cried. "Half the school is looking for you. When you hadn't been on a bus, or seen at the railway station, and your aunt said you hadn't gone home . . . oh, Frue, why did you do it?"

I drew back, trying not to cry like a baby. "I lost my way in the wood. I was going to catch a Farmer's bus on the road and go to London."

"But why? Because you were unhappy? Look, I must tell them I've found you." And she yelled, "Miss Dook, she's here! Safe!"

Miss Dook's voice came back: "Thank goodness!" Then she blew a whistle and shouted, "Girls . . . everyone . . . she's found!"

They were all waiting in a snow-filled clearing. Miss Dook, Mademoiselle (a bit different from Paris?) and some Senior girls. I learned later that others had gone to different parts of the wood.

Miss Dook looked me over briefly and told me to follow as quickly as I could. It was the only way to get my circulation going. She strode away and the others followed, glancing back at me curiously. Nicola stayed by my side and held my arm. I was so stiff with cold that I needed help at first.

"But why did they let *you* come?" I asked, when I was feeling warmer with the effort of struggling through deep snow and underlying mud. Miss Dook seemed to know the way all right. We were on a main path that I suddenly recognized by piles of cut timber, almost covered with snow.

"I got around Dook," Nicola said, and her hand tightened on my arm. "Look, Frue, Mrs. Hailey-Reed told us. I hope you won't mind. About your father and mother only a few weeks ago, and how you were at a stage school in London. And then I knew . . . I always thought you looked familiar. I saw you in that play in the West End last year."

"You mean she told the whole school?" I could well imagine the scene; Mrs. Hailey-Reed telling my sad story. But in a way it was a relief that they knew, if only they wouldn't talk about it.

"Well, not the Juniors. She was upset, you see, when you were missing, and she knew you hadn't been very happy. The whole thing was awful for you, and I do understand better than some. *My* mother didn't die, and I was unhurt, but she was buried for hours and I *thought* she was dead. We've been bombed twice in London. Mother has a wartime job and my father's in the Army. Look, Frue, can't we be friends?"

We had reached the wooden gate at the end of the wood. Beyond was only a snowy field, then the five cedars of Hartsthorn House. The others were still ahead, though Miss Dook often looked back. Without really knowing her at all, I was suddenly sure that I could like Nicola better than any girl I had ever met.

"If you can put up with an idiot who runs away and makes a mess of it," I said.

"I can put up with an idiot," she answered, and laughed, and pulled me on faster. "Come and have some disgusting warmed-up lunch."

"Mrs. Hailey-Reed will scold me first."

"She'll swoon over you, dear child. With relief. She's a bit much, but I like her, and Hartsthorn has its brighter side. It's gorgeous in good weather, and spring *will* come."

Mrs. Hailey-Reed did indeed greet me with great emotion, which was embarrassing. I would almost have preferred to be scolded and punished. But she was nice, really, and did seem to understand some of my problems.

I ate the "disgusting warmed-up lunch" by the fire in the Tudor Room and then went to bed. I slept until the others came upstairs to get ready for dinner. They crept in, but relaxed when they saw I was awake, and I must admit they were very tactful, without being in any way awkward. They asked how I was and told me the little happenings of the afternoon. But Richenda, the last to leave, lingered for a moment by my bed.

"You were an ass, you know," she said. "If you felt like running away you might have done it properly. You could have taken the footpath across the park to Hartsthorn Common; then the woman at the lodge couldn't have seen you. I suppose you wanted to get back to the Lennox School? Mrs. H-R told us you were offered a scholarship there, but your aunt wouldn't let you take it. It must be a much more interesting place than this dump, especially when you're used to all the excitements of London and have even been on the stage."

"I did want to see Madame," I admitted. "But I did behave like a fool. She would only have sent me back."

"Well, make the best of us, dear child," she said, half-mockingly, but in a very friendly tone. "You were sadly missed. Annabella was in floods of tears. She dotes on you. Did you know?"

"It's only because we talked together on the first day, and she's such a miserable little thing."

"Oh, don't apologize. She *is* a miserable little thing, and you seem to have been kind to her. No one else has bothered with her much. She's too young to be here. But I've told off the Juniors to be nicer to her." She waved and hurried away as the bell rang. Nicola came in as she went out.

139

"I heard you were awake," she said. "Mademoiselle's on dinner duty and I'm going to beg her to let me bring up your tray, and one for me, so that we can eat together and talk."

"Oh, do!" I cried. The snowy woods seemed like a dream by then, but she had said we must be friends. In spite of the cold air in Gallery Room, for the very first time Hartsthorn House did not seem the bleak place I had thought it.

My tongue released, I told Nicola as much as I could about my London life, even something about the night of the rocket, and the time at Dogwood House. She seemed particularly interested to hear about Aunt Mildred and Muriel, and laughed over my comments on country life as it had first struck me.

"I felt the same when I came here two years ago. It's different for a lot of the others. Large country houses, with horses and all that. I'm a Londoner, too, and I was there all the time until 1943. But Mother always wanted me to come to boarding school, and I love it now. This Chiltern country has a strange kind of spell. But I suppose you don't understand."

"Oh, yes, I do," I said. "I *have* felt it. I want to see some of the really old places on the hills. I'm going to explore in the holidays, but here we're stuck. Imprisoned."

"It seems worse in this weather," Nicola said. "Sometimes we go for long walks and cycle rides."

She had to go away to do an hour's preparation after dinner, and only when she had left me did I remember that I had always felt I had seen her before. Funny that she had felt the same, and it was because she had seen me in the play. We *couldn't* have met, as she lived in Bayswater and not in Chelsea.

I lay there listening to the snow against the windows, and the weird sounds the wind made in the old house.

After that I did begin to settle down at Hartsthorn. Nicola's warm friendship made all the difference. We learned that we could laugh at the same things, and there was an extra bond because she knew London so well and had always been taken to the theatre. I liked all the girls in Gallery Room, now that I had nothing to hide and could talk freely, and to my surprise they actually begged for stories of the Lennox and my brief acting experiences.

The story of the making of *Traveler's Joy* turned out to be a winner. They were fascinated that I remembered the house when the family lived there, and demanded every detail I could recall about the film. Richenda wrote about it in her letters home, and her father replied that he remembered the film well. "It was a little gem," wrote Lord Neston, "and Fruella Allendale showed remarkable promise as the ghost child."

Richenda read the words out to everyone in Gallery Room, and I must admit that I basked in their interest, though there was an element of sadness and frustration because any promise I had shown was in abeyance while I was at Hartsthorn House. The "me" they had first known wasn't the real Frue Allendale, and gradually I began to enjoy myself. I did little bits of acting after the lights were supposed to be out, and once or twice I danced in my petticoat, raising my bare arms in ballet movements. I even gave a ballet lesson, which ended in frantic giggles and brought Matron's wrath down on our heads.

Even the horrors of Hartsthorn didn't seem so bad now I had friends. Scraping the plates and washing them in half-cold water was almost bearable while talking hard to Nicola or Jemima.

The first time I went to Dogwood House for a weekend Aunt Mildred was grimly disapproving of my attempt to run away and, as the snow had melted, promptly set me to digging the kitchen garden. But I had time to walk in the village. It was heavenly to be out alone, and Muriel gave me some sweet coupons, as mine were in Mrs. Hailey-Reed's hands.

It was lovely to eat delicious, well-cooked meals, and Katie welcomed me joyfully, saying she had missed the young company. The village people welcomed me also, speaking as if I had been away for a long time, rather than a few weeks, and I heard all the latest gossip. But to my surprise I felt lonely in my gable room, and the village gossip wasn't as interesting as the real or imagined affairs at Hartsthorn House. Where Mademoiselle went in her spare time was a more interesting topic than the Red Cross sale of work, and the rows between Dook and Short were more dramatic than a story of stolen eggs.

I seemed to have grown very absorbed in my life at Hartsthorn; yet, at the back of my mind, were always thoughts of what was happening in London, where occasional rockets still fell, and I *longed* to hear from Paul. I pinned all my hopes on seeing him again in the Easter holidays. I had had two letters from Mrs. Tremartin, in which she said Paul was absorbed in his work. Paul was the one secret I had kept from Nicola. After all, there was so little to tell.

Aunt Mildred was as busy as ever, but I was struck by how gaunt she looked. Muriel was very quiet; more remote even than usual. She was the center of the one startling thing that happened during that first visit.

I took a stroll on Sunday afternoon, before walking back to school for the five o'clock deadline, and I decided to go and see Robert. Aunt Mildred was lying down, and Muriel had disappeared. I walked quietly toward the buildings of Little Hartsthorn Farm, and suddenly I drew back behind a round hayrick. For Muriel and Robert were standing in the great doorway of the barn, apparently in deep conversation. There was something about them that made me feel I must not intrude. They were both standing sideways to me and Muriel was looking up at Robert. And, all of a sudden, something about her face stabbed me to the heart. I had seen that look before. It had been on my mother's face when my father came home before Christmas.

It was an immense shock. Muriel . . . *Muriel*, nearly forty years old, looking at a man like that. I knew—was sure—that she loved Robert.

I went away very quietly, hoping I had not been seen. I liked Muriel and I had always felt it was very sad that she was unloved. But I had thought it was far, far too late for *her* to love, even if there had been anyone suitable. And now . . . Robert was some years younger, he was an earl and must have a son, and there was that attraction in London.

She *loved* Robert the Earl. As I walked back up the lane

I thought how tragic it was, and I wondered if Robert knew. He must only think of her as someone older, whom he had known all his life.

When I was back at school I told myself that I had imagined it, and hoped I had, because there must come a day when Robert married, and then how would my cousin feel?

In early March there were the first feelings of spring. One or two days were almost warm, and it was a delight to walk in the woods and find the first growing things. There were winter aconites on a bank near the house, and tiny green shoots everywhere. Rooks began to build nests in the high trees by the church, and it was no longer so icy cold in Gallery Room.

Muriel had lent me her camera and, though films were scarce, along with everything else, I took two rolls of pictures of the house and some of the girls. There was a good one of Nicola.

I went to Dogwood House once more before Easter and Robert came to dinner. I watched covertly, but there was nothing to see, for Robert talked mainly to Aunt Mildred and Muriel was quiet, as usual. She did not even look at Robert much; was that significant? I thought maybe I would try not to look at Paul in company.

The conversation was, as usual, about affairs in the Hartsthorns, but there were occasional references to the war, which still dragged on. Not long now, everyone said. The Germans were beaten, but the Japanese would take longer. I could not imagine a return to a world where there was less fear, and fewer privations, but

144

spring was coming very fast. Soon it would be holidays.

Before term ended we cleaned most of the house. It was really great fun, for we were let off lessons for two days, and even the members of the staff donned overalls and tied their hair up in old scarves. I was lucky, for I worked mostly in the banqueting hall, the Tudor Room and the Captivity Parlor, and there was pleasure in making those ancient rooms more beautiful. Annabella attached herself to me and really worked quite hard; a funny little figure in a too large overall. By then I had almost forgotten she was the daughter of a duke; it seemed of little significance. Lord Neston's girl was doing a horrible job in the kitchens, and the daughter of the Earl and Countess of Heswall, an important Senior, was violently washing the long kitchen passage.

We had a three weeks holiday over Easter. Richenda invited me to spend a week with her, but Aunt Mildred refused to let me go on the grounds that it was too far for me to return alone on the overcrowded, delayed wartime trains.

"I'm glad you've made friends with Lord Neston's girl," she said to me, when I arrived back at Dogwood House. "But I'm sure they'll ask you again when things are better."

I was glad not to go. I liked Richenda, but still found her a bit overpowering. Now if it had been Nicola . . . but Nicola lived in a small flat, the only accommodation they had been able to find after being bombed for the second time, and there was no room for visitors. I did suggest to Nicola that I might ask Aunt Mildred to invite her to Dogwood House, but I was surprised, and a little hurt, when she seemed embarrassed and said I had better not. Sometimes Nicola's manner puzzled me; I had the vague feeling that, though we were such good friends, there were times when she drew back. When she was going to say something and didn't.

Aunt Mildred knew about my friendship with Nicola, and she asked quite a lot of questions about her. I enjoyed talking about my friend, so didn't mind.

Aunt Mildred had bought me a secondhand bicycle, which she said I could take back to school with me. Meanwhile I cycled far afield on the quiet country roads, sometimes leaving the bicycle to explore. Wherever earthworks or mounds were marked on the map I did my best to find them, though it often meant a long scramble. Robert lent me a book that was a great help.

The Chilterns were beautiful in the springtime, with primroses, wood anemones, and many other flowers I couldn't name. The first delicate green beech leaves were unfurling and the woods were full of birdsong. But I was very lonely. I wrote to Paul about my discoveries, though pride told me I ought not to do so, as he had clearly forgotten me. A postcard came in a few days from Wiltshire, where he was working on some kind of "dig." The only words of comfort were scrawled at the bottom of the card: "Keep your chin up. See you again."

I knew, after that, it was no use going through the village just as the morning bus was due. He wouldn't come soon.

I grew despondent again and bored with the tasks Aunt Mildred constantly found for me. London seemed a million miles away. I read Nicola's letters hungrily, though she did not sound very cheerful herself. The last rocket base had been found, and so there was no danger from the sky, but food was short and everything seemed dreary in spite of the spring. But she had been to two plays and three concerts.

"I miss you, Frue, and even all those nutty folk at Hartsthorn. I'm looking forward to getting back to school."

So why hadn't she wanted to stay with me? Aunt Mildred would probably have liked to meet her, though she might have been more impressed if Nicola had been aristocratic. She really *was* impressed when a letter came from Annabella with a coronet on the back of the envelope. Poor little Annabella; she was lonely, too, at Mollington.

"Please, Frue, come and stay with me in the summer holidays," she wrote. "Daddy wants to meet you."

The summer holidays! How long would the interlude last, I sometimes asked myself in rebellion and despair. I had learned a great deal; I knew far more about people than I ever had before, I loved the country and didn't mind outdoor work. But my real work was in abeyance. I tried to talk to Aunt Mildred about the Lennox, but she wouldn't listen. She brushed my arguments aside.

"Leave it, Frue. Leave it. I know there's no danger in London now, but let's get the war over first. You really are an ungrateful girl. I send you to one of the best schools in the country and you're discontented."

"I'm not ungrateful, Aunt Mildred," I said unhappily. I didn't want to hurt her feelings; in a strange way I was beginning to like her. "Hartsthorn's quite fun now that

147

I have friends, but I ought to be getting on with my career."

I wouldn't have been so lonely if Muriel had been more companionable. Once or twice she came out cycling with me, but her mind seemed far away. I supposed she was thinking about her hopeless love for Robert. One evening they both took me to the cinema down in Missencombe, and I sat between them, loving the film but thinking of them some of the time. Grown-up people were so puzzling.

I knew they met often. Muriel was frequently over at the farm. But the rumors of "the attraction" were now stronger in the village. Robert had been to London several times, and not to the House of Lords, either.

"You mark my words," I heard Mrs. Clare saying, as I entered the shop. "There'll be a wedding up at Great Hartsthorn Church come the summer."

"But who is she?" I dared to ask, and they all fell silent, staring at me covertly. I was sure they didn't know.

On my last night at home I heard Muriel crying. I was thirsty and went to the bathroom for a drink of water. It was three o'clock in the morning, and the crying sounded terribly desolate. I didn't know what to do. Would she hate me if I went in? Would it be tactful to go back to bed and forget it?

I opened her door softly and slipped into the room, closing it behind me. Moonlight slanted across the floor. "It's only me," I whispered.

The sobbing stopped. "Go away, Frue!" she said, quite savagely.

I was really scared, but I didn't obey. I had cried

enough in the night myself to know how awful it was. I sat down on the edge of her bed and said, "If you would like to . . . to talk to someone, truly I can keep secrets. I promise never to tell a soul."

"Oh, don't be a fool!" she snapped, and buried her head in the pillow. Well, that wasn't talking to me as a child. Encouraged for no very clear reason, I leaned forward. It was quite a cold night, with a touch of late frost, and I was shivering.

"Look, I don't know, but is it Robert?"

She shot upright, nearly knocking me off the bed.

"Robert! Is the whole village talking about it?"

"No. No." I was more scared than ever. "Of course not. I saw your face once when you were talking to him, and I thought. . . . Oh, if it's true, I'm so *sorry*. It must be awful to love someone who doesn't love you."

Muriel was silent for so long that I began to think she would never forgive me. I could see her face in the moonlight, but it told me nothing. Somewhere in my mind I was thinking that if suffering went on forever—even until one was nearly forty—then I would never bear it.

Then: "What makes you think he doesn't love me?"

"Oh, well, the village *does* talk. They know he has someone in London. And so . . ."

She was shaking. She seemed to be laughing silently, but tears were pouring down her face.

"This blessed village! The someone in London is an old aunt who recently lost her husband and can't manage her affairs. Robert's being very good to her. You've got it all wrong, Frue. Keep it to yourself, and I'll tell you."

"I've already promised," I said shakily.

"Robert *does* love me. He first asked me to marry him nearly six months ago. There's no one else."

I was totally taken aback. No, I did not understand grown-up people, or anything about love.

"Then . . . then why?"

"Because I'm a hopeless coward," said my cousin Muriel.

13

Blue Birds Over

Thoughts ran wildly through my head. The wedding up at Hartsthorn Church would be Muriel's; she would be a countess and, far more important, loved and happy. The more I knew Robert the more I liked him. He was gentle, nice, and funny most of the time; with just a touch of astringency, as when he told me about the horrors of Hartsthorn House. A marriage between Robert and Muriel seemed, suddenly, perfectly possible and right.

"I don't understand," I said finally.

"Well, think of it," said Muriel, speaking very quietly, but bitterly. "I'm five years older and a nobody. The whole countryside would rock, and I can't face it. Besides, I can't face my mother. She needs me. She's said often enough that I'm past the marrying age. She'd laugh at me, or be desperately upset. She hoped long ago that Molly might marry him, but it never crossed her mind that I might. I'll be thirty-nine in October. Robert could have anybody, only he won't look. I *am* a coward, but it isn't only that. I don't think he *should* marry me."

One thing at least was clear to me. "Oh, what does it matter what anyone thinks?" I asked. "They'll get over it. And as for Aunt Mildred, why she'd be delighted to have you marry an earl. She's a bit of a snob. And she's often said Dogwood House is too large and too much for her. She could live with you and Robert at the farm."

Muriel gave a muffled snort. "You make it sound so easy, Frue. She'd say a great many cruel things, and so would the whole neighborhood, not to mention a good part of the rest of the country. Robert may seem to live in obscurity, as an ordinary farmer, but every newspaper and glossy magazine in Britain would be onto it with claws out. I've told you, and now try to forget it. It won't happen. For his good, largely. I won't make a fool of him. Now go back to bed. You're frozen. We won't speak of this again. Good night."

In the morning she was pale and very composed and went off to clean out the hens. Aunt Mildred was in a snappy mood and said several very sharp things to her at lunch. I could think of nothing but the strange story I had heard in the night. It *would* take courage to face the breaking of the news of an engagement; that was clear enough to me. Even if Aunt Mildred didn't, other people might well say awful things. What about that strapping girl who would give Robert children?

But I had learned a good deal at Hartsthorn House. In many ways, in spite of their silly talk about the gardening boys, the girls were much more sophisticated than the ones I had known at the Lennox. Or at least more ready to discuss openly things that had been talked about secretly in London. Whether it was horses or people, they took birth for granted and talked about it naturally. Miranda had had a new little sister just before term ended, and her mother was forty-three. Jemima had an aunt who had married for the first time at forty and who

152

had given birth to twins ten months later. At the time I had just thought it a bit strange and somehow not very suitable, but now it was significant. Even a son might not be impossible if Muriel married Robert.

Had she thought of that? What was going on behind her controlled, pale face?

Frustrated, I had to go upstairs to change into my school uniform and a taxi came for me at three o'clock. That time I went alone, and how different it was to drive uphill in the brilliant sunshine to a world that I knew. Nicola was there already, bending over her box in the outer hall, and she greeted me with the news that she was in Gallery Room now as Marilyn Blakely had left unexpectedly and Matron had given her the vacant bed.

Mrs. Hailey-Reed received me in the Tudor Room with a slightly dramatic hug and kiss and the words; "Well, dear Frue! Back to the nest! And your friend Nicola will be with you in Gallery Room. Isn't that splendid for you both? *Such* a nice girl, though her parents are quite obscure."

"Mine are nonexistent," I said, for sometimes snobbery stuck in my throat, and the pain of my parents' death had faded a little, so that I could even mention them.

"Oh, my dear!" said Mrs. Hailey-Reed. Her hair was brighter blonde than ever. "We value you for your talented little self."

"And because Robert spoke for me," I thought, as I retreated to the banqueting hall, where Annabella hurled herself at me. She looked smaller and paler than ever. With her was the duke, just turning away from Mademoiselle, who was receiving the new arrivals.

153

"Frue! Oh, Frue!" Annabella cried. "Daddy, this is Frue!"

"I hear how kind you've been to Annie," the duke said to me, smiling. "One day I hope we'll see you at Mollington. Annie speaks of you constantly."

A divorce was going through between the duke and duchess and I had seen it hinted by gossip columnists during the holidays that she would not be given custody of Annabella.

The duke was quite a good-looking, youngish man, but I saw how tired he seemed. His eyes were a trifle bloodshot and he had deep lines on his face. The gift, or curse, of extra observation that had been born in me on New Year's Day had never really died. I noticed how anxiously and tenderly he looked at his daughter and I forgot the things Aunt Mildred had said and answered as warmly as I could:

"I've done my best, but of course Annabella is very young and not with me often. If it would help to have me in the holidays, I'd be glad to come."

"I think it *would* help," the duke said, and smiled at me and led Annabella into the Tudor Room.

I rushed away to carry my things upstairs, glad that my trunk was in the outer hall and not in the kitchen passage. As we all put away our possessions, talk flowed continuously in Gallery Room. In the middle of it I suddenly met Nicola's eyes and we both smiled in a secret, understanding kind of way. Oh, it was good to be with someone who seemed really my own; my own friend, whom I had sadly missed.

I wished I could tell her about Muriel and Robert, but of course it was impossible. By early dinner I felt I had been back at Hartsthorn for days; yet I couldn't quite forget the conversation in the night, and Muriel's problem. I felt sadly sure that she would not marry Robert, and yet that was absurd, if that was what he wanted. "He could marry anyone, but he won't look." So Robert knew what he wanted, and it was silly and wrong, surely, to refuse to face Aunt Mildred and the gossip columnists. If I were only older and wiser I might be able to help.

Aunt Mildred and I met nowhere, but I knew by then that she wasn't the laughable caricature my father had thought her. She did a lot for other people, and even, maybe in a misguided way, for me. It was true that she need have done nothing more than keep me for a week or two. I'd had my place at the Lennox, and if I could have kept my part in the play I would have been earning. That play was still running, one of the successes of the West End stage. It might run for a year or more, and when I remembered that I felt very badly about my lost chance. All the same, I did somehow like Aunt Mildred.

After her fashion she had been kind, even remembering to buy me a bicycle. She might *not* say cruel things to Muriel and Robert; she might even be genuinely glad, snobbery apart, or snobbery included. Only how could I convince my cousin of that, especially when I was again incarcerated in the nunnery?

But the nunnery was a great deal better in the summer term. We were outdoors a good deal, and the light evenings made everything seem more pleasant. Sitting at my desk in one of those drawing rooms, supposedly absorbed in my preparation, I would glance as often as I dared through the long windows at the vast view. For the East Front had a view straight down the Stretch, and, as April gave place to May, the delicate green, lighted by the evening sun, was so beautiful it hardly seemed real. Never before had I seen the spring in the country. The hawthorn was in bud and there were lilacs already out here and there, and wonderful hanging tassels of laburnum.

So much beauty made me sad, but really there was not much time for solitary dreaming. We worked, played tennis, walked in the woods, and cycled far afield. The food was still awful, there were still cockroaches and mice, but enchanting light filtered into the banqueting hall, where great sprays of lilac began to appear under the historic portraits.

It was May and the war was ending.

"Tomorrow! Tomorrow is VE Day!" cried Richenda. "Mrs. H-R says it will be a whole holiday and we'll take a picnic lunch out with us."

So the war in Europe was over. Those long years that had started a day or two after we returned from Cornwall were going to be part of history. Another world of peace was being born, and there really would be those mythical blue birds over the white cliffs of Dover.

I found it almost unbearable. Maybe some of the others did, too. So much had gone forever, so many people would never know that the struggle was almost finished. Japan was still not beaten, but Japan seemed far away.

I felt bitter as well as sad. My father might have lived to make those films he had dreamed about but for that rocket fired from another country and falling arbitrarily in Chelsea. My mother might have worn lovely dresses bought in a store and been there always with us.

But they had both gone, and I found it hard to rejoice on that day in May when the whole school, and most of the staff, carried picnic lunches through the woods and over the hills, to eat them on the edge of the ridge, where the Vale of Aylesbury lay far below, green and lovely in the sun.

After lunch, when most were still sitting in groups, talking, I slipped away alone. And I sat on the hill's edge, lost in flowering dogwoods and spindle trees, and tried to come to terms with the fact of peace. Down in Missencombe they would be holding street parties, flags would be flying, people singing. But I think I had never felt so desolate and alone since that morning more than four months ago, when I heard the street musician playing "It's a Lovely Day Tomorrow" as I stood, shivering and sick, outside the Regent Palace Hotel.

Tomorrow is a lovely day . . . and tomorrow had come.

"Frue!" It was Nicola. She sat down beside me.

"I'm not good company," I said, for in a way I didn't even want Nicola then. "It's all over, nearly over, and I wish I were dead. I know I'm sometimes dramatic, but at the moment I do mean it. If I were dead like all those other people who were killed fighting, or in the bombing, I wouldn't have to go on now. Somehow all this beauty makes it worse; the little flowers in the grass, those cuckoos calling down in the vale."

Nicola stretched herself out beside me on the short grass and didn't answer for several moments. Then she said, "It *is* sad. I know how you feel. I lost a young cousin in the Battle of Britain; he was twenty-one. I was only a child then, but I planned to marry him. I used to pray he would wait for me, until I grew up. Then I heard he

157

was dead, shot down in flames. He *wouldn't* have married me, of course; he was eleven years older. But I wish he was alive and knew we had won the war. You aren't the only one, Frue. Most people lost someone, or their homes. Mademoiselle's thinking of Paris, and Mrs. Weston is sitting alone not far away. Her husband is safe and will come home; they'll be happy again. But she lost her father and mother and younger sister during the bombing of a Northern town. Didn't you know that?"

"No, I didn't know." Oh, why did the cuckoos call so loudly and joyously down there? "But she still has her husband. I have no one but Aunt Mildred and Muriel, and they aren't really in my world."

Nicola didn't answer. Her hand was hanging down into a little chasm where the white chalk of the hillside was exposed. Her face was slightly turned from me and I studied it curiously. Dark hair falling back from a good brow, a short nose, rather prominent cheekbones. Familiar . . . something about her face . . . the awareness had haunted me vaguely from my very first glimpse of her, though I had never mentioned it. Then I saw with shock that she was crying. Tears began to pour from under her half-closed lids and roll down into her ears.

"Why, Nicola!" I gasped. Tears in the night; a face seen in moonlight.

"I'm sorry, Frue. I'm being dramatic, too. It *is* a sad kind of day, in spite of the rejoicing. And you have a way of talking . . ."

"I'm too sorry for myself," I said absently. I was still studying her face. "Do you know, I've always wondered of whom you remind me. It's my cousin Muriel."

158

She rolled over and sat up, tossing back her hair. "Frue."

"You have the same bone structure, but now I remember. During the first days I was at Dogwood House I saw a kind of family album. There was a picture of Muriel when she was about your age, and one of Molly, too. I told you; the Molly who ran away."

At that point I was merely interested; I hadn't got it. But she said, "Yes, I know. In the holidays I told Mother about you, and she said I might tell you when I thought fit. Mother's name is Molly, and . . . well, we're some kind of cousins. I knew that from the first. Well, your great-aunt is my grandmother. I suppose it's cousins."

"You *knew?*" Suddenly I didn't mind the cuckoos, or the trees around us, glorious in May. She had always seemed my kind of person, my real friend, from that night when we had danced in the banqueting hall. Of course you weren't always close to relations, so maybe it wasn't that. But even a remote tie of blood seemed to make an extra bond. It was a sudden small miracle.

"I asked about you soon after you came. They told me you lived with your aunt, a Mrs. Butler of Dogwood House, Little Hartsthorn. It wasn't a coincidence, you know, that we met in the Chilterns. Mother always loved this country, though she ran away from it. She looked around for a school for me and found Hartsthorn House. Now you know why I was so interested in your Aunt Mildred."

"So Molly didn't starve in a garret," I said, still a bit winded with surprise.

"Of course not. Did your Aunt Mildred think so? We

aren't rich, but my father was an architect before he joined the Army, as I've told you. He was quite successful, and soon he'll start again. Are you pleased, Frue?" She looked at me anxiously. "I couldn't stay with you in the holidays. It wouldn't have been quite honest."

"Pleased!" I had never been demonstrative, but suddenly I hugged her. We rolled over and nearly fell into the little chalky chasm. "It's like a story," I said. "But won't Molly—your mother—come back? Won't she get in touch with Aunt Mildred? Was there such a bad quarrel that it can't be patched up?"

"Oh, I think it was one of those build up things. They never got on, and Mother decided to escape. The thing that made her feel bitter was that she wrote to her father and said she'd like to keep in touch, but her mother overrode him and said Mother had gone and that must be the end of it. By what you've told me about your aunt, she's a pretty dominant character, and rather unbending."

But Aunt Mildred was old now, she had had cancer, and possibly old quarrels were unimportant.

"Couldn't we see Aunt Mildred together and tell her?"

"Not yet. Wait. The war's over and Mother always said she'd give up her job as soon as Father came home. Now we've met, and are friends, I think it will work out in time. I believe Mother will be glad when she has time to deal with it. It depends on Aunt Mildred."

My great-aunt Mildred . . . her grandmother. Beyond the trees, along the hill's edge, they were shouting for us. It was time to go. Suddenly tomorrow was indeed a lovely day. I didn't want to die. I would go on, I would work and strive and get back to the Lennox, and have

Nicola and her mother as well. Only, right now, I was at Hartsthorn House, and we had to walk back through the woods and end that VE Day with a dance in the banqueting hall, under the portraits of Queen Elizabeth and Robert Speen.

When we approached the house there was Muriel just propping up her bicycle against the white fence near the West Front. She was wearing rather a pretty summer dress and sandals. When she saw me she lifted a large box out of her bicycle basket and advanced, smiling. My eyes went from her to Nicola. They were as alike as if they were mother and daughter. If I had not realized it an hour or two earlier, I believe I would have known it then.

"Katie baked you a Victory cake, Frue," Muriel said. "You can share it with your friends. She even found some colored candles."

It had been a strange, emotional day and I almost burst into tears. I wasn't alone; even Katie cared enough to remember me on that day the war ended in Europe.

"Oh, please do thank her very, very much," I said, holding the box against my breast. "Muriel, this is my friend Nicola. Nicola, my cousin Muriel. You've both . . . heard about each other."

Maybe the strangest moment of that day.

It was all the stranger, somehow, when Muriel said without really looking at her, "How do you do, Nicola? I hope we'll see you at Dogwood House one day soon. And now I must fly. Robert and I are going down to Missencombe as soon as he's finished the milking. They'll be dancing in the streets tonight."

She mounted and rode away past the church and down

the driveway, and Nicola and I looked at each other.

"So that's my aunt!" Nicola said softly. "What a nice face she has. She's better looking than Mother, I do believe. But she looks tired. There are dark circles under her eyes."

Oh, poor Muriel! Probably she wasn't sleeping well. But I couldn't tell Nicola why she was unhappy.

"Is that Robert the Earl she's going with to Missencombe?" Nicola asked, as I didn't speak.

"Yes," I said. "Yes, Robert the Earl."

\14/

Aunt Mildred Surprises Me

Soon after VE Day Mrs. Hailey-Reed called the whole school together in the banqueting hall.

"Now, girls," she said, "since we've been at Harts-thorn we have given a play outdoors at the end of every summer term. And it's time we made plans for this year. Many of you have been studying *A Midsummer Night's Dream* in class, so I've decided that this shall be the play. We have a lot of talent here, and I'm confident that we'll put on a good show for all our visitors. We'll stage it on the lawn beyond the cedars. There will be plenty of parts, even for the Juniors. All we shall need is a lovely summer's day. Of course, if it's wet it will have to be performed in the gym."

"It never is wet, Mrs. Hailey-Reed," said Richenda, and Mrs. Hailey-Reed laughed and touched the ancient paneling. "Forgive me if I say 'Touch wood!' "

I was dismayed. I longed to act again, but not in an amateur production at school. It would only make my loss more painful. Nicola, who understood how I felt, could offer no comfort.

"They're sure to give you a big part," she said. "You stand out head and shoulders above everyone else when we read scenes or poetry."

Most of the main parts went to Students or Seniors, but I was given Titania. Miranda was Puck, and Annabella, Peaseblossom. She had taken private dancing lessons while at Mollington, and was a lovely little dancer. To see Annie dancing was to forget the miserable little child in a too big hat.

I went to Mrs. Hailey-Reed in the Tudor Room as soon as I saw the list. She listened to my halting plea to be let off, then threw up her hands. "What a selfish girl! Here am I with the gift of a real actress, and you say you won't do it. Think again, dear Frue, think again!"

Selfish? Maybe I was, always thinking of my own feelings.

"I'd rather not," I said brusquely. The thought of the play still running in London was a knife in my heart. The girl who had once understudied me had been offered the same part when a film was made later in the year.

"Oh, my dearest child, that's not the way to speak to me. How important good manners are! I pride myself that all my girls have good manners and are never awkward. How can girls go out into society, into the *world*, unless they've learned to conduct themselves with grace?"

"The only place where I may have to conduct myself with grace, Mrs. Hailey-Reed," I said, "is on the stage."

She laughed and pulled me to her. She was using some very sophisticated scent.

"And who's going to Mollington?" she asked playfully.

I disentangled myself with "grace," at least I hope so. I had been invited to Mollington for the first two weeks of the summer holidays, and Aunt Mildred had accepted the invitation with delight.

"I don't eat peas with my knife," I said. Sometimes Mrs. Hailey-Reed really made me feel prickly. Hartsthorn House was such a mix-up; half the girls would be presented at Court, but they had to spend a lot of time scraping plates and even sweeping that cockroachy kitchen passage.

She laughed. "You are not a garden boy, dear Frue. And you will be my Titania, won't you?"

I was her Titania. Once I got started, I began to enjoy it. Any acting was better than no acting, it seemed. And really, Hartsthorn House was a very pleasant place in summer, especially with Nicola as my constant companion. Since discovering we were related we seemed to have grown closer together.

"You two might be sisters," Richenda said once.

June came, then early July. The woods were thick by then, many of the footpaths overgrown with brambles and high nettles. There were flowers everywhere on the hills, and I learned to know their names. The rare Chiltern gentian was a find, and I loved the little patches of wild candytuft, thyme, and marjoram on some remote hill's edge.

When I was back in London, as I had to be some day, I would miss the country. But London drew me all the time with a dreadful longing. The "interlude" had become very pleasant, but it had to end some time.

Mrs. Tremartin wrote that, by some miracle, the house and studio were being repaired and they hoped to move back early in September. Paul was in his last term, and very busy. He must be; I had heard nothing from him since the postcard. He had forgotten me.

So many things seemed to be in abeyance. My "real" life, Muriel and Robert, the fact that Aunt Mildred still did not know about Nicola and Molly. We had no half-term at Hartsthorn, but I went to Dogwood House for two short weekends. Muriel seemed to avoid me, and Aunt Mildred looked very gaunt and rested more. On my second visit she startled me by asking abruptly:

"Frue, tell me the truth. Are you settled now at Hartsthorn?"

We faced each other. Her eyes were steady and enquiring.

"I'll never be settled there, Aunt Mildred," I said. "Oh, I like it. It's lots of fun, in a way, and the teaching is so good. They're all nice in Gallery Room, and Nicola . . ."

"You're fond of this Nicola Kelsey?" Fancy Aunt Mildred even admitting one could be "fond" of a friend.

"Yes," I said.

"But you'd go back to the Lennox School?"

"I *have* to go back to the Lennox," I told her. "Soon I'll be sixteen. I'm missing everything."

"You talk nonsense," said Aunt Mildred, and walked away.

Nicola and I often talked about how we could reunite the two families. "It's so silly," I said. "Someone must make the first move, and your mother is the one who knows."

"She's too busy to bother now, I think," Nicola said. "The war has taken it out of her. I'll talk to her in the holidays."

The war! The war with Japan still went on, and, in spite of peace in Europe, there were still endless shortages, maybe more than ever. But our soldiers and airmen were coming home. The only girls who were still desperately worried were those who had brothers in Japanese prison camps. But most at Hartsthorn were too busy with exams and the play to give much thought to the outer world.

The future, after the play and the end of term, held my visit to Mollington, then the rest of the summer at Dogwood House. A lonely summer, with no young companions. I tried not to think of it.

Then the miracle happened. I had been sent over to the flat above the old stables with a message for Mrs. Weston. It was a Saturday morning; hair washing was going on at the house and some girls were playing tennis. When I left the flat I walked a little way along the driveway, glad to be alone. And, coming rapidly along the drive, was a tall, long-legged figure wearing a blue shirt and gray trousers.

I stared, completely unbelieving for a moment. That winter morning was far in the past. I had thought I might never see that figure again. But here was Paul in summer, coming toward me!

I ran. Not two ballet dancers advancing slowly that time. Unashamedly, I ran straight into his arms. We collided quite violently and he held me.

"Steady!" he said. "I do have luck! I thought I'd have to face your Mrs. Hailey-Reed before I saw you. *And* seventy girls. Where can we go to talk?"

"What about the church?" I suggested.

The church was cool and silent. I had grown to love

it for its beauty and historical associations, though I had never grown to like the services we had to attend. We sat in a back pew. I could hardly believe in Paul's presence.

"You look fine, Frue," he said. "I didn't know you were so pretty. Being suntanned suits you."

I didn't know what to say, so I just looked at him. He seemed taller and thinner than ever, but he looked much better than he had done in the winter. There was no face on earth I would sooner have seen.

"You're a country girl now?" It was a question.

I answered, "Look, I'm still a city girl at heart, but I do like the country now. I don't even mind working in Aunt Mildred's blessed kitchen garden. Things *grow*. I never saw anything grow before. You don't notice in London."

"Hum!" He sat sideways in the pew, looking at me so closely it was a bit embarrassing, but nice. "Well, that's good. That's why I've come. To see if you'd like to work really hard on a farm during the holidays. Mother suggested it. She said, if you'd care about it, she'd write and ask your Aunt Mildred. You see, we're going back to Cornwall for two weeks in August, to work in an Agricultural Camp. All the lot of us; Father, Mother, and me. You know that farms still need all the help they can get, with the men coming back so slowly, and there's the harvest and everything. The Government runs these places. Actually, we chose one that isn't a *camp*. We'll all be accommodated in a big old house on the hill above Penzance."

Cornwall. And to be with the Tremartins for two whole weeks. I wouldn't mind working myself to the bone in the Cornish fields.

168

"Oh, yes, I'd love to go! But I'm going to Mollington for two weeks when term ends to keep Annabella company. I told your mother about her."

It seemed it would fit perfectly. Mollington was in Northern Kent. I could travel up to London that Saturday morning, be met by one of the Tremartins, and go straight on to Cornwall by train.

"But Aunt Mildred will never let me," I said sadly.

"She may . . ." The church door opened with a loud creak and a dramatic voice boomed, "Frue, dear child! Hiding here with a boy! How *could* you? You know how carefully . . ." It was Mrs. Hailey-Reed.

Paul leaped to his feet, falling over a hassock. I rose also, feeling my face blushing fiercely. I had forgotten the rules of the nunnery in my sheer joy at seeing Paul. Mrs. Hailey-Reed did tend to guard us from the male sex. Richenda said it was because a girl of sixteen had once eloped from Hartsthorn and had been caught in a London hotel saying she was nineteen. As she was a very important girl, and the affair had made the newspapers, Mrs. Hailey-Reed had never got over the scandal.

But this was different. "Mrs. Hailey-Reed," I said, grasping at dignity, "this is Paul Tremartin, whom my aunt knows. He came from London to bring me a message about the holidays from his mother. And I happened to meet him when I was sent on a message."

She calmed down and greeted Paul graciously. "But you should have come straight to me, children. Let us go back to the house, and Paul must have some coffee."

She led us both into the Tudor Room, and everyone who saw us gaped with interest. It would be all over the school in five minutes that I had a young male visitor.

169

The secret of Paul was out all right, but I would say he was a family friend.

Mrs. Hailey-Reed talked to Paul with her maximum charm, and he, having recovered, talked well. But we had no more private conversation, for she saw him off herself and sent me up to Matron to have my hair washed.

I could think of nothing but the joy of that brief meeting, and of the possibility of going to Cornwall with the Tremartins. I must write to Aunt Mildred at once and tell her how much I would like to go. Only I was afraid she would never agree, and then the lonely holiday weeks would seem worse than ever.

Paul had not forgotten me; he had said I was pretty. When my hair was dry, I looked in a mirror and saw my eyes shining and my cheeks flushed and thought that really I did look quite nice.

Oh, Aunt Mildred, let me go to Cornwall! But I felt I knew her well enough to be sure she would not let me go so far away with people she hardly knew. She might not mind the hard work; she was always trying to "toughen" me.

It was Aunt Mildred's birthday one week before term ended. I knew because Muriel had told me. I had painted her a picture of Dogwood House, taken from a photograph, and Nicola, who was good at woodwork, helped me to frame it. I had found I was quite good at art. I planned to pack the gift carefully and post it, though I was rather hating Aunt Mildred again because I had heard nothing at all about Cornwall. It must be all up and she had refused.

Then, two days before the birthday, Mrs. Hailey-Reed called me into the Tudor Room and told me that I was to be allowed to go home for a few hours to celebrate. Aunt Mildred wanted me there for dinner on her birthday, and Robert would drive me back afterward.

"Be here not later than nine-thirty, dear Frue," she said.

The girls were all envious. A good dinner, and Robert the Earl to drive me home, seemed to them the height of bliss. I was divided in my feelings; I would hear bad news about Cornwall, but I would see Robert and Muriel again. I often thought of them, and longed for them to be happy, but clearly nothing had happened.

There was a footpath down the broad reaches of the Stretch that cut off half a mile. I walked alone through that July afternoon, my feet brushing through grass and flowers. The curves of the hills were golden with ripening oats and wheat, but faintly dimmed by haze. The heat was thundery and the air so still that the swish of my passing sounded loud.

I walked along the lane from Hartsthorn Bottom, passing the gates of Robert's farm. And there was Robert, talking to a man who was mending a fence. Robert's face was very tanned, but it looked thinner. He looked rather thin altogether, and I wondered if he was suffering because Muriel wouldn't marry him. If *I* loved someone I would marry him whatever the circumstances and not care what the world thought and said.

"See you at dinner, Frue!" Robert called.

The dogs rushed to welcome me. By then I had grown used to them, and even rather liked them. Encircled by dogs, I ran around to the back of the house; in country fashion, we rarely used the front door. Muriel was pull-

171

ing lettuces in the kitchen garden and waved. Aunt Mildred was talking to Katie in the kitchen. She seemed to have aged a great deal; she even stooped, which she had never done before. But her manner was as brisk as ever.

"So here you are, Frue! You look very hot. Katie has made you some lemonade. That nasty synthetic stuff." There were no lemons in wartime.

I said "Happy birthday!" and gave her the picture. I carried the lemonade into the drawing room, and she followed me. She was going to tell me I couldn't go to Cornwall. I felt a little sick with heat and apprehension. Until then I had kept a shred of the dream. I could hardly believe it when she said, "I thought you might as well come down and have dinner. We shan't see much of you during the first month of the holidays. First Mollington, then Cornwall."

"Aunt Mildred!" I gasped. "May I go to Cornwall, then?"

"You may," she said shortly. "It's all fixed. Mind you, you'll come home with a broken back from constant bending in the fields. I believe they work people pretty hard. But it all helps toward the country's recovery, and I hope I'm patriotic enough to realize it. Your fare will be paid by the Government, and I'm told you'll be paid for the work you do."

"Oh, *Aunt Mildred!*" I was so astonished and happy I choked over the lemonade. "You *are* a surprising person. I thought you must have refused long ago."

"Hum!" Aunt Mildred eyed me with amusement. "You have a lot to learn about human nature, Frue. Open-air work never hurt anyone. Better than that sickly world of the theatre."

I let the sickly world of the theatre slide. First things first. Paul for a fortnight, in Cornwall. Of course there would be an element of sadness to be back in that countryside I still well remembered. Moonlight at Kennack Sands, kittens in a farmyard, the voice of doom on the radio. Long, long years ago.

By dinnertime the sun was sinking in a strange, thick glow, and it was hotter than ever. There was just no air at all. The summer woods brooded, seeming nearer than usual. The lowing of a cow across the valley was extraordinarily loud.

Muriel and I helped Katie in the kitchen. It was far too close to eat a hot meal, so there was to be chilled soup, cold duck (Robert had sent the duck), salad, and strawberries to follow. Our own strawberries miraculously grown in the garden. I had never seen them growing before.

Muriel seemed edgy and snapped at me when I dropped a lettuce leaf on the floor. When she went out of the room Katie whispered, "Take no notice of *her*. She isn't herself."

"Do you know why?" I asked, looking closely at the old woman, but she gave me a blank look back and didn't answer.

Muriel changed into a green dress and put on more lipstick than I had ever seen her use before. She was just ready when Robert arrived, looking very hot. The sunlight had gone, and purple-black clouds seemed to rest on the opposite hill. Maybe it was the coming storm, but there seemed to me a lot of tension. Yet it was all quite civilized. The meal was delicious and Aunt Mildred and

Robert talked as usual. Muriel didn't eat much and never once met my eyes. It was all pretty strange, somehow.

Then there was a violent crash of thunder, and lightning played over the valley, eerily illuminating the woods and the curving cornfields. It was almost a relief, as if our tension, too, had broken. Soon the rain was pouring down in torrents and the world was almost black, except when the lightning flashed.

At nine-fifteen, when I should have returned to school, Aunt Mildred telephoned Mrs. Hailey-Reed to say I would have to stay at home until morning. Robert would drive me up in time for breakfast.

Then Robert said he must go, as some of the buildings might be flooded and the animals would be scared by the storm. Aunt Mildred lent him an old raincoat to put over his head and he dashed out to the car and drove away through several inches of water, while we stood in the porch, watching, until he was out of sight. In spite of the storm it was not much cooler, though there was a gorgeous smell. I wished I could have gone back to school. Something about Dogwood House was making me uneasy.

We returned to the drawing room and Aunt Mildred asked Katie to make some more coffee. Muriel stood by the window, eerily lit by the lightning. Aunt Mildred said sharply to her back, "For heaven's sake, Muriel, come away from the window!"

Muriel swung around abruptly and said she was going to bed.

Aunt Mildred looked her over coolly and came out with the staggering curtain lines:

"I've had enough of this nonsense. Make up your mind to marry the man. We'll have no peace until it's settled."

\15/

The Reunion

It would have made a splendid ending to the second act.
I had sunk down into a deep chair, and, from there I
waited breathlessly through a long silence. The silence
was broken, not by Muriel but by a roll of thunder.
Though the storm was moving away, it still had strength
in it.

Even when there was comparative silence again
Muriel did not speak. Aunt Mildred said, "Lost your
tongue, have you?" just as if Muriel were nine and not
nearly thirty-nine.

Oh, no, I did not yet know my Aunt Mildred, and
clearly Muriel did not know her own mother.

"How did you know?" she asked finally. She was very
white, her dark eyes huge. Oh, it was dramatic, and
exciting, and wonderful, too, because it was going to be
all right.

"Know?" Aunt Mildred snapped. "I'm neither blind
nor in my dotage, and I haven't believed that village
gossip for at least three months. Robert told me himself
that he goes to London to help an old aunt with her
affairs. And one day I suddenly knew how things were.
If ever I saw anyone acting like a lovesick cow you have
been, but he's been nearly as bad lately. I'm an observant

woman and I've seen the looks he's given you when he thought no one was watching. He always was a bit weak, and maybe he needs a woman older than himself. And you're healthy. You could still give him a son. So why the hesitation?"

Plain words, harshly spoken. Cruel, in a way, yet oh, how marvellous! I could almost have clapped. It was the best play I had ever watched; yet more than a play, because I was involved.

I wanted so much for Muriel and Robert to be happy, and, yes, I almost loved Aunt Mildred then.

"I hadn't the courage," Muriel said slowly.

"Courage? Rubbish! Everyone will talk, but what does that matter? Give the gossip columnists a field day; it will soon die down. You've no time to lose, so get on with it. I suggest the end of August for the wedding. And don't let out the date. It can be quite a quiet affair."

"With Frue as my only bridesmaid?" Muriel sounded faintly hysterical, but her face was quite different; alive and glowing.

"Of course. She can wear her blue dress and carry late roses. So that's settled." Katie came in with the coffee, and Aunt Mildred poured out for all of us, telling Katie to get an extra cup. "Muriel is going to get engaged tomorrow, Katie. You can drink her health in coffee."

"The Lord be praised!" Katie cried piously. She was not surprised and she did not ask to whom.

"But stop! Stop!" Muriel ordered. "Mother, what will you do? The farm's big, and Robert has said . . . there's the little east wing. You and Katie . . ."

"Maybe later," Aunt Mildred answered. "Katie and I will stay here for a time. After all, you'll only be a few

176

hundred yards away. Oh, I know I said I needed you, but you'll still be in Little Hartsthorn. Give me the pleasure of talking about my daughter, the Countess of Hartsthorn."

That, at least, was in character. I laughed, and they both remembered me.

"Frue knew?" Aunt Mildred asked. "Well, she has eyes, too. It's the village that has been blind. You tell Robert in the morning before he takes Frue up to school, and he can send the notice to the *Times* for the next day. Then we'll ride it out."

"There'll be something to ride," Muriel said.

"So what?" Aunt Mildred asked. "That vulgar Americanism is useful sometimes. Get on up to bed, Frue. You won't sleep after all that coffee and excitement, but try."

I went up to my gable room. The rain was still falling, but softly, and the thunder was rumbling far away. Oh, what an evening! Thank heaven for the storm, after all. If I had gone back to school I would have missed all the drama. Muriel and Robert were going to be happy; Aunt Mildred might be happy, too; and *I* was going to Cornwall with the Tremartins.

We always arose early at Dogwood House. Muriel went over to the farm at seven o'clock and came back in the car with Robert. They both looked radiant.

I said to Aunt Mildred, as I stood in the porch to say good-bye, "Will you be coming to school for the play?"

"We'll all come," she said.

"Mother's coming for the play," Nicola told me, later that day. Until then I had mostly monopolized what

177

conversation we had managed, telling her about the events of the previous evening.

"So they'll meet," I said, and apprehension swept over me. So much had been resolved, but how terrible if the meeting between Aunt Mildred and Molly was a failure. They might not even meet, of course, in what would probably be a large crowd, unless we planned it and introduced them. Though, even after so many years, Aunt Mildred could hardly fail to recognize her own daughter.

The *Times* was one of the few newspapers we were allowed to read, and the notice duly appeared the next day. Mrs. Hailey-Reed saw it at once, and gradually the whole community knew that my cousin Muriel was going to marry Robert the Earl. The whole countryside knew it, but I missed all the disruptions at Dogwood House. I was lost in the life of Hartsthorn, as the last days of term passed quickly away. Final rehearsals, frantic last minute alterations to costumes. There were several dressing-up boxes at Hartsthorn, and parents had helped where they could. Miraculously some lovely costumes had been created. The weather forecast was: Sunny, very hot.

The day after the play was breaking-up day. I was to go straight to Mollington with Annabella, while my trunk was sent direct to Dogwood House. Muriel delivered two suitcases for me in a taxi. Muriel, with a diamond engagement ring and a happy face.

"You take both of them with you to Mollington," she said. "We've put your old things in one, for Cornwall. Boots, and strong shoes, and most of the things you'll need farming. Matron will help you to decide what to take to Mollington, and they can send it back to Dog-wood House at the end of your stay."

"I'll manage," I said. "Are you happy? No need to ask, really."

"Yes, but it's been tough," she told me. "Wait until you see the glossies. The newspapers went to town, but the magazines will be worse. The photographers were awful. But Mother was splendid."

The day of the play was perfect summer. We spent the morning arranging the "stage," with a backdrop of the cedars. The Juniors carried out every chair in the house.

By the time of the last rehearsals I'd been rather ashamed to realize how much I was enjoying the play. A school play was such small beer after the West End of London. Yet the play was good. Mrs. Hailey-Reed pro-duced it herself, and she knew what she was doing, no question. There was knowledge behind her direction; maybe that tale of her having been in the chorus was true. Or of course her experience might just have come from putting on a play at Hartsthorn every year.

By two-thirty the visitors were beginning to arrive. Petrol had been found from somewhere, for most par-ents came in their own cars. A few arrived in taxis from the railway station.

Nicola and I were in a state of nervous excitement as we lingered on the gravel by the West Front. Her mother was expected by train and taxi.

"Oh, what if it doesn't work out?" I cried. "What if Aunt Mildred won't speak to your mother? What if your mother still holds those old grudges?"

"I don't think she does," Nicola said. "I think she'd be glad to be in touch again. Why, here she is!"

Mrs. Kelsey was very nicely dressed, in spite of short-ages. She was so like Muriel that it was uncanny. When Nicola introduced me to her, she hugged me in such a motherly way that I felt quite choky.

"Frue, dear! Nicola has told me so much about you. I'm very glad you girls have met and made friends. We're part of your family, you know, and I plan to see a lot of you just as soon as the war is really over and we can get a larger flat."

In the seven months since my tragedy no one had spoken to me quite like that. I knew suddenly that, in spite of what had happened, I was rich. Aunt Mildred, Muriel and Robert, the Tremartins, and Nicola and her mother. But, while I was thinking this, Robert's car swept around the corner and drew up beside us. Aunt Mildred got out first, and so fate brought her immediately within a foot or two of Molly. Nicola and I gripped hot hands. It was an awful moment. A good deal of my future happiness depended on this meeting.

By then I knew that Aunt Mildred could be surprising, but, even so, she astonished me. She looked Molly over closely, then said, "Well, Molly! We meet again. I hoped we would. It seems only sensible when our girls are such good friends."

"Aunt Mildred!" I gasped. Even in the excitement I noticed that she thought of me as *her* girl.

Mrs. Kelsey blushed like a schoolgirl. "Mother!" she said weakly. "Aren't you surprised?"

"Not a bit," Aunt Mildred said briskly. "Why should I be? Your daughter is exactly like you and Muriel at the same age. Frue brought home photographs in the Easter holidays. She never stops talking about Nicola, and don't forget I had heard your married name. You were just married when you wrote to your father. I wasn't sure if Frue knew, though."

"Not until VE Day," I said. "Oh, I'm glad! Is it all right?"

Aunt Mildred and her daughter exchanged glances, and Aunt Mildred said, "As far as I'm concerned it's very much all right. I haven't the least doubt that we still won't see eye to eye on many things, but I hope I'm forgiven, Molly. Muriel, come and greet your sister. Robert, this has turned into a family reunion."

The next few minutes were a bit chaotic. Everyone was talking at once. But I did hear Molly say to Aunt Mildred, "But . . . are you ill, Mother?" and Aunt Mildred answered briskly, "Of course not. Why should I be ill?" In spite of the heat, a little chill fell on my heart. Aunt Mildred looked so gaunt and pale.

Then we all began to walk toward the lawn. Molly said to Muriel, "I've heard you're going to marry Robert Speen." She lowered her voice. "He's better looking than he used to be. I hope you're both very happy. I always felt guilty over leaving you to bear the whole brunt at home."

"I didn't need to stay," Muriel said.

"No, but I knew you. You stayed, and it must have been tough sometimes." She looked around at the great house dreaming in the heat haze, at the cedars and the beautiful short grass. "When we used to come here as children for the Christmas party I never thought you'd be mistress of the place."

"I never shall be," Muriel said quietly. "We'll never live here. I shall just be a farmer's wife."

"Funny farmer's wife! A countess. What strange things the war has done. But it has brought us all together again."

The war. . . . It had taken away my parents and my old life. It was not over yet. It was Thursday, July 21.

I had to run away to put on my Titania dress. I wished I could stay there to hear the talk as the guests were given cold drinks on the lawn before the play, which was to start at three-thirty. In the second intermission there would be tea.

Annabella in her fairy costume came to my side just before the play started. We were hiding in the shrubbery near the gym.

"Oh, Frue! Tomorrow we'll be at Mollington. I am so glad you're coming."

Dear heaven! I had forgotten Annie. I should have added her to my list of riches. I knew she loved me, and I was very fond of her, however I had felt about important families way back in that bleak January.

Annabella, the fairy, was almost pretty. Her part in the play had given her some standing among the Juniors, who now seemed quite kind to her, accepting her as one of themselves.

"A lot of wonderful things have been happening, Annabella," I said. "I'll tell you all about it in the holidays. Now it's time for the play to start."

We had done our cleaning of the house a week before, and there was nothing to do on the last morning of term but eat our breakfast (pretty awful) and wait for the various transports to take us away. Many of the girls, including Nicola, Annabella, and I, were going in relays to the station and were to be escorted to London by Dook and Short. Others were to be picked up by parents, who had spent the night at hotels in Missencombe. The Duke of Mollington had attended the play but had driven home afterward. Dook and Short would put us on the Mollington train at Charing Cross, for we had not wanted to miss the dance in the banqueting hall that had ended the festivities.

There were not many Missencombe taxis and we had to await our turn. I escaped from Annabella and the rest and wandered into the banqueting hall. Roses were everywhere, adding to the strange, sweet smell of polish and freshly oiled paneling.

It was so beautiful; the heart of a great historic house. I was aware, then, that it was a privilege to know it so intimately. I even forgave the cockroaches and the mice.

I stood under the portrait of Robert Speen. That Robert Speen who had died for the Parliamentary cause, giving up his peaceful country life to do so, as John Hampden had done, however misguidedly. We had heard both sides of the argument in history classes.

I was startled when a hand fell on my shoulder.

"Saying good-bye to us, are you, dear Frue?" asked Mrs. Hailey-Reed.

"It's very beautiful," I said, wondering why she sounded so emotional. I wondered at the same time if Muriel's son, if she had one, would look like the man in the portrait. There was something called genes, and he might look like Muriel. But he ought to look like the Speens, down the centuries.

"So it is. Well, have a good time, dear child. You'll be a great help to poor Annabella, I know. And then the

183

war work. So splendid, working on a farm in Cornwall. Don't forget us, dear Frue."

Nicola and Annabella were calling for me. It was time to go, but only for seven weeks, of course. In the autumn I would be back.

"Good-bye, Mrs. Hailey-Reed," I said, and I fled over the polished floor to the outer hall and the waiting taxi.

16

Traveler's Joy

The two weeks at Mollington were fascinating, but a little sad. The castle was wonderful, very ancient and almost surrounded by a moat. But the Army had occupied all except the West Wing for nearly five years and, inside, there was not much to suggest former grandeur. Annabella was a very nice little companion, though I missed older company. I tried not to let her guess how much I was looking forward to going to Cornwall.

The best part was having dinner with Annabella and her father. The duke knew a lot about the theatre and we found plenty to talk about. Sometimes, after Annabella had gone to bed, we were still talking.

The day came when I went to London and then to Cornwall. Trains were still delayed and terribly overcrowded, with little food and no comforts, but I enjoyed every moment of that long journey. Paid for by the Government, I had no need to feel guilty when I saw that awful poster demanding if my journey was really necessary, and it was splendid to be with the three Tremartins again, especially, of course, Paul. It really was traveler's joy, that time.

It was sunset before we passed through Marazion and saw the dream island, St. Michael's Mount, and a short while later we reached the terminus, Penzance.

The house on the hill above Penzance where we were billeted was very old; an old Cornish manor house. We were a varied bunch of people; of all ages and from all walks of life. The Tremartins and I were assigned to a farm at Paul, the village after which Paul had been named. It was high on the cliffs above Mount's Bay, and from the fields I could look over the water to St. Michael's Mount and, beyond it, to the Lizard Peninsula. Around Lizard Point was Kennack Sands. But I didn't have time to look much, because I was mostly gazing down at the earth, hoeing turnips or harvesting potatoes.

We were expected to work very hard, for long hours. I wondered if the farmer knew he had a famous artist among his farm workers. Mr. Tremartin worked tirelessly, and Mrs. Tremartin seemed in her element. She said it was wonderful to be back in her native place, and such hard open-air work was a change from the tensions of London.

Paul and I worked together. My hands were soon very dirty and sore, but I was wildly happy. We talked as we worked, and I had soon forgotten all shyness. The superior young man of the London days seemed far away. We were friends, we began to know each other. It didn't matter that I was not yet sixteen. Somehow I felt almost equal.

On August 6 the Americans dropped an atomic bomb on Hiroshima and, on August 9, on Nagasaki. We heard the news on the radio in the evenings, and it was horrific, but it all seemed remote, when we were in Cornwall, in summer.

On August 14 Japan surrendered unconditionally and

the war was over. Over! Finally and forever. August 15 was VJ Day and many of the workers defected and went away to enjoy themselves. It was a powerful temptation, there was so much Paul and I wanted to see, but we went to work as usual in those high fields, and we worked all day in the hot sunlight.

On Saturday we would go home, and how I wished we could have stayed longer. I had got into the swing of things and no longer minded my rough hands and aching back.

On the morning after VJ Day there was a letter from Aunt Mildred; a large envelope, in which another envelope was enclosed. I took it to work with me unopened and read it during our first tea break. Aunt Mildred's letter filled me with astonishment.

> Dear Frue,
>
> I hope you have found the work in Cornwall rewarding and not too tiring. Plans for the wedding are going ahead quietly, and Muriel and Robert will be married in Great Hartsthorn Church on August 30. You may be pleased to know that Nicola is going to be the second bridesmaid.
>
> On the day of the play, after I had talked to Molly, I told Mrs. Hailey-Reed that you would not be returning to school. Molly has said you can have Nicola's room at the flat, and, in any case, they hope to get a larger place soon. I personally regret it, but you seem to mean to continue with your acting career, so you are to return to the Lennox in September. I hope you are pleased, and will spend some of your holidays at Dogwood House or at the farm.
>
> We look forward to seeing you again on Saturday.

187

Take a taxi from the station.
The enclosed letter came for you yesterday.
Your affectionate
Aunt Mildred

I could hardly believe it. The interlude was over. I would go back to London and return to my old world of the theatre. To my great surprise, regret was mingled with my joy. Hartsthorn House was part of the interlude and it had gone forever. Never again would I sleep in Gallery Room; never again would I wander in the banqueting hall, lost in its beauty. I would not be there to see the beechwoods aflame with autumn tints, and I would miss the great Christmas party, when yule logs burned in the huge fireplace and the girls sang carols from the gallery. Unless, oh, unless I could get back to Dogwood House in time and go with Robert and Muriel.

Nicola would miss me, but we would meet often in the holidays; she could stay at Dogwood House. Annie would be bereft, but she was accepted by the Juniors now, and maybe I would go back to Mollington.

I didn't open the other letter until our lunch break, when we were sitting in the shade of an earthen bank. The envelope bore the name of my father's solicitors. It told me that the film, *Traveler's Joy*, had been bought by British television, for an early showing when the service started up again and, as I owned the main rights to the film, most of the money would come to me. There was also a chance that it would be bought by American television.

"I believe," wrote Mr. Shaw, "that you can thank Lord Neston for this. He has much influence, and it seems he well remembers the film. When we have the contracts we will be in touch again."

Traveler's Joy, that film made in the Chilterns in 1939 that I had thought almost forgotten.

"Know people of influence," Aunt Mildred had said, and I had resented it. But the reissue of the film would mean that I wouldn't be wholly dependent on my relations.

On our last night in Cornwall, Paul and I walked in a remote lane high above Penzance. I felt sad, because it had all been so wonderful, being with the Tremartins in the high summer fields.

"Everything has worked out well for you, Frue," Paul said. He took my hand and we walked on slowly.

Well. . . . Yes, all was well, except that Father and Mother were dead.

"I'll miss you," Paul went on. "But we'll meet. We aren't going to let you go now."

"You'll be at Oxford and very grand," I said.

"Not all that grand. A scruffy undergraduate. Look, Frue, you're only a kid . . ."

"Sixteen soon," I reminded him. It was an enchanting evening, warm and still. From our high lane we could see the bay and the Scilly Isles steamer just entering the harbor.

"Yes." There was no one around. He pulled me to him and kissed me; a proper kiss, on the mouth. "You'll be a famous actress . . ."

"Who said?"

"And I'll be a famous archaeologist. But listen . . ."

"I'm listening," I said shakily.

"You'll grow up. Remember that. The twain might

meet. We could work it out somehow."

"We can try," I said, suddenly violently happy.

We might both meet other people; as the years passed love might be found in other places. But Paul was the one I wanted. I had known that months ago, in another life.

It was almost dark as we walked back down the lane, and the town lay dimly below. Cornwall had somehow sealed the years; before and after.